MYSTERY AT MARIAN MANOR

Mystery
at
Marian Manor

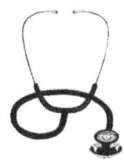

*The Adventures of
Nora Brady, Student Nurse*

M. E. ROCHE

Mystery at Marian Manor: The Adventures of Nora Brady, Student Nurse
by M. E. Roche

Mystery at Marian Manor: The Adventures of Nora Brady, Student Nurse
copyright ©2008 by M. E. Roche

All applicable copyrights and other rights reserved worldwide. No part of this publication may be reproduced, in any form or by any means, for any purpose, except as provided by the U.S. Copyright Law, without the express, written permission of the copyright owner.

This is a work of fiction. Names, characters, places and incidents either are the product of the author's imagination or are used fictitiously. Any resemblance to actual events, locales, organizations, or persons, living or dead, is entirely coincidental and beyond the intent of either the author or the publisher.

NOTE: Product names, logos, brands, and other trademarks occurring or referred to within this work are the property of their respective trademark holders.

Cover Art by M. E. Roche ©2008

Address comments and inquiries to:
http://www.meroche.com

Paperback ISBN-13/EAN: 978-0-61589-953-4

Library of Congress Control Number: 2008929144

Printed in the United States of America

First Edition: 2008

Second Edition: 2013

For Mom,

my first and

favorite nurse

and for

Dad

who introduced me

to the magic of

the written word

Acknowledgments

Thanks to my friends and family for their feedback and support. A special thanks to my niece Meghan and to my grandson Kyle for their belief in possibilities.

The Florence Nightingale Pledge

I solemnly pledge myself before God and in the presence of this assembly to pass my life in purity and to practice my profession faithfully. I will abstain from whatever is deleterious and mischievous, and will not take or knowingly administer any harmful drug. I will do all in my power to elevate the standard of my profession, and I will hold in confidence all personal matters committed to my knowledge in the practice of my calling. With loyalty, will I endeavor to aid the physician in his work, and to devote myself to the welfare of those committed to my care.

Prologue

The old woman awoke with a start. Breathless. Heart pounding. Something was wrong. She lay still and waited for her eyes to adjust to the dark. Slivers of moonlight filtered through the drapes making the bureau at the foot of her bed look like a subterranean troll. She took a deep breath to calm herself. "It was that second dessert tonight," she thought. "Too much sugar, too close to bedtime. It's not like me to be so jittery. I wonder what time it is?" She lifted her wrist only to discover that she wasn't wearing her watch. "What happened to my watch?" She tried to turn over in the bed, but she was weak and when she lifted her head, she felt dizzy. She knew she needed help.

She searched for the call light, but it wasn't tied around the side rails where she usually kept it. When she did find the light and tried to pull it closer, she lost her grip. She heard it hit the floor. Maybe someone else heard it fall, but she knew that wasn't likely. There were only a few staff here in Marian Manor at night and if they were in another resident's room, they wouldn't have heard anything. She lay still for a moment, thinking. She gave herself a pep talk. "Now, Harriet, pull yourself together," she said. "You're an engineer, for heaven's sake. This problem is right up your alley."

She tried to call out for help, but her throat was dry and her voice was hoarse. She tried again to reach for the call light and thought she felt the cord near her shoulder. If she could at least get the cord, she could pull it up. She lifted her head again and tried to turn on her side to reach the cord, but the dizziness overcame her. She felt sick to her stomach and there was a burning heaviness in her chest. Before she had time to wonder what was happening, she was dead.

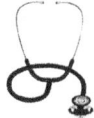

Chapter 1

Tina Kunz flew into the nurses' station, late again, strands of her short black hair trailing out from under a baseball cap. A pair of roller blades were tied together and flung over one shoulder. Her uniform scrubs were grass stained at the knees and the palm of her left hand was bruised and bleeding. She also had a large scrape on the palm of her right hand, but she didn't seem to be in pain, only in a hurry.

"Tina!" I exclaimed. "Are you O.K.? You're late. Jean's upset and Deborah's called in sick."

"I'm fine, Nora," she said, stashing her roller blades under the desk and quickly washing her hands at the sink. "I'm cross-training for that marathon next week and I thought I had enough time. I'll take care of Jean." Grabbing some Band-Aids and a clipboard, she plopped down on the stool next to mine.

"Can you help with these?" she asked, as she held out her hands, palms up. Her head nodding towards the Band-Aids she had tossed on the counter.

"Sure," I replied, reaching for the Band-Aids. Tina was one of my best friends, but sometimes I had to think she lived in a different world. A world that didn't recognize the fact that she and I were second year nursing students at Marian Manor, with a boss and an instructor that liked us to be on time for our assignments. We liked Marian Manor, a two-story, white monstrosity of a nursing home, surrounded by beautiful gardens, on the outskirts of Jacobsport, a small coastal town in northern California. We also liked Jean Newman, our head nurse. Most of the time.

"Tina! In here! Now!" said Jean, stepping out from her office doorway. Tina jumped up and followed Jean back into the office. Despite the fact that Tina towered over Jean by a good four inches, it was clear who was boss.

The office door was closed for only a minute. When it opened, the staff heard the tail end of Jean's scolding. "Tina, you really test my patience. You could be such a good nurse, but you'll never make it if you don't learn to get here on time. It's not fair to your co-workers when you keep them waiting." Jean opened the door as she said this and signaled the night nurse to begin report.

"I'll work on it," said Tina. "Really, I will." She didn't meet my eyes when she sat down this time.

"Melba Jones never slept last night," said Ruth Rice, the night nurse, "but we couldn't figure out why. "We tried her sleeping pill, turning her, and then a pain pill. Nothing seemed to help." Ruth was experienced and very thorough. She could be somewhat gruff, but we knew if she was concerned about something, it was important to follow up.

"Melba hasn't been herself lately," said Jean. "I'm worried about her too. Nora, let's talk with Dr. McCain today. See what he thinks."

After Ruth's report, Jean got up and walked over to the assignment board. She erased Deborah's name. Deborah was one of the R.N.s on 2 West, our unit. Our job, as students, was to follow one of the regular nurses around for several days and then we would have our own assignments. We were on a work/study program for three months and Mrs. Floyd, our nursing instructor from Del Norte State, would check with Jean once a week to be sure we were learning what was required and that we weren't being treated like slave labor. I was always anxious to be on my own. I looked forward to being a full-fledged nurse, but that was at least two years away. Graduation couldn't come soon enough. With a nurse calling in sick, we were certain to have more responsibility. I was probably the only one who was ever happy about a sick call.

Jean re-worked the room numbers next to our names. "It's the best I can do with Deborah being sick again," she said. "Dominic, I want you to work between the two teams and be sure to get the guys in 205 down to breakfast first. Any questions?"

There was a quiet groan, but no one said anything. We knew that Jean had done her best in pairing the nursing staff. I was working with Lonnie. Not my favorite person. She was slow and I just didn't trust her. I liked working with Dominic. He and I were a good team. We each knew how the other worked and what we liked and didn't like. We got things done quickly.

I guess Lonnie didn't trust me either because she seemed to do everything her own way. When I asked her to do things, she didn't listen to me. If I tried to correct her, she got angry or ignored me. I knew I was only a student and I knew I should be able to learn from everyone, but Lonnie could have been the exception. It would be a major problem if we worked together very often.

"If everyone is settled," said Jean, "I'm going over to 2 East. One of their residents passed away last night."

"Who was that?" I asked. I sometimes worked extra over on that unit and I knew some of the residents.

"Harriet Allen," said Jean.

"I didn't know she was ill," I said.

"It was unexpected," said Jean, turning down the hall.

I liked Harriet and was sorry to hear that she had died. I wondered what had happened, as she always seemed in good health. I looked over at Lonnie. "I guess we'd better get started," I said. "Will you please check a temp and blood pressure on Mrs. Jones in 219, first thing? I'll be along as soon as I get my med cart."

Lonnie nodded, but she didn't look at me. I pulled my medicine cart out into the hallway and collected my keys from the medicine room. We keep medicines locked up at all times.

Herman Jessel, one of my favorite residents, was coming down the hall. I could see that Herman was dragging his right leg again and I knew he was in pain. His buddy, John Parker, another favorite of mine, was close behind. Each was using his walker as we had been encouraging them to do for safety.

"Nora! Thank goodness you're here today!" said Mr. Jessel. "I know you won't give us any lectures about the evils of drink." Both Mr. Jessel and Mr. Parker were 89-years-old. The two men shared a room and they shared a liking for one small glass of whiskey first thing in the morning and last thing at night.

The two friends looked like brothers and, oddly enough, they had the same birthday. Tall, but stooped, each had a full head of beautiful white hair which was always carefully trimmed. And the men were quite proud of the fact that each had his own teeth.

"How's my favorite nurse this morning?" asked Mr. Parker. He always asked the same question, no matter who the nurse happened to be. I liked hearing it, even if I was only a student.

Mr. Parker and his wife had come to Marian Manor about five years ago with serious medical conditions. Mrs. Parker had died shortly after that and as Mr. Parker had no children and no other relatives to help him, he had stayed. Mr. Jessel had been at Marian Manor for nearly ten years. After his wife died, he, too, needed some help because of his medical conditions. While he had plenty of family in Jacobsport, he liked his independence. He and Mr. Parker had become close friends.

"I'm doing great," I said, pouring the two small glasses of whiskey, "and you two look good this morning." The two men clinked glasses, downed the shots quickly, and set the empty glasses on my cart. "Mr. Parker, how about something for that leg of yours this morning?"

"The leg is fine, Nora," said Mr. Parker gruffly.

"I don't like to complain," said Mr. Jessel, changing the subject, "but that nurse who was doing the pouring yesterday, knows nothing."

"She tried giving us those plastic cups," said Mr. Parker. "Everyone knows that plastic spoils the taste of a good whiskey."

"And she tried to tell us that whiskey wasn't good for us!" said Mr. Jessel. "Let's just see if she's around at 89!" The two men nodded in agreement, and then continued on to the dining room where the smell of fresh coffee and bacon was calling me as well.

I decided to check on Mrs. Jones and Lonnie before I started my med rounds. As I walked into Room 219, Lonnie was taking Mrs. Jones' blood pressure. Mrs. Jones slowly turned her head towards me and I could see the distress in her eyes. She was a thin, black lady who weighed less than ninety pounds. Sometimes she was confused. Her wiry gray hair was now sticking out from her head in all directions. There was a fine sheen of moisture on her face and her lips were moving, but there was no sound.

Lonnie handed me the vital signs on a slip of paper. Everything looked O.K. I sat down at the side of the bed and took Mrs. Jones' hands in mine. "How are you doing, Mrs. Jones?" I asked. "We're worried about you." Mrs. Jones kept her eyes on me, but she didn't answer. "Can you tell me what's wrong?" No response. "Are you in pain?" She shook her head and kept her eyes on me. After several strokes, communication and movement was difficult for Mrs. Jones. I didn't know what to do. I didn't know what she needed. "Do you want me to call your daughter?" I asked. This time she nodded her head. "I'll do that now," I said as I got up. Squeezing her hands and stroking her forehead, I promised to come back.

Once in the nurses' station, I placed the call to Mrs. Jones' daughter, Tanya. "Mrs. McCluskey? This is Nora, the student nurse who is with your mother today."

"Is everything O.K.?" asked Mrs. McCluskey.

"Your mother's O.K.," I replied. "It's not an emergency, but we've been a little worried about her these past few days. Apparently she didn't sleep well last night and she doesn't seem to be herself this morning. She wanted me to call you. We also planned to call Dr. McCain."

"I'll come as soon as possible," said Mrs. McCluskey. "I'll just need to reschedule a meeting." Tanya McCluskey was the mayor's administrative assistant.

I put down the phone and walked back to tell Mrs. Jones the news. Lonnie had just finished getting Mrs. Jones into her high-backed wheelchair with the head support.

"Lonnie, is everyone else up for breakfast?" I asked.

"No, Nora," she exploded. "I've been tied up in here."

"I know that," I said. "Tell me what still needs to be done and I'll help." It was going to be a long day if I had to keep helping Lonnie in addition to my own work.

"I haven't gotten to any of the rooms at the end," said Lonnie.

When I went down to the end of the hall, I found those residents had finished dressing. After helping them walk to the dining room, I was getting my medicine cart when someone called my name.

"Are you Nora?" asked a pretty, black woman standing by the nurses' station. She was wearing a well-tailored purple suit and beautiful amethyst earrings.

"Yes," I replied. "You must be Mrs. McCluskey." I extended my hand.

"Well, let's see if we can figure out what's going on with my mother," said Mrs. McCluskey. "Where is she?"

"She's in the dining room for breakfast," I said, thinking that Mrs. McCluskey's "take charge" manner must have worked very well down at City Hall.

"Great!" said Mrs. McCluskey. "She needs to get up as much as possible."

As we walked into the dining room, Mrs. Jones' eyes brightened. Mrs. McCluskey pulled up a chair next to her mother. She bent and kissed her mother's cheek. Then she took her mother's hands into her own and gazed into her mother's eyes. "Hi, Mom. Nora tells me you seem to be worried about something. Can you tell me what's wrong?"

Mrs. Jones looked over at me and then back at her daughter. Slowly, and in a hoarse voice, she said, "Wing."

Mrs. McCluskey looked at her mother intently. "Wing?" she repeated. "I don't know what you mean, Mom."

Mrs. Jones closed her eyes for a moment. Then she opened them wide. "Wing, wing, wing," she said excitedly.

Suddenly, I understood. "I think she's trying to say 'ring,'" I said. The problem with speech was part of the strokes that Mrs. Jones had suffered.

Mrs. Jones nodded her head, and her eyes brightened as she looked at me. Then she looked down at her hands. "Wing ... wing," she said again.

Tanya McCluskey looked puzzled and then the light went on in her eyes as she gazed at her mother's hands. "Her rings are gone!" she exclaimed. "Her wedding ring and her engagement ring. They're both gone."

As I looked down at Mrs. Jones' hands, I realized that Mrs. McCluskey was right. I felt sick. Everyone knew about these rings. How they had been in the Jones family since the Goldrush. Sapphires and diamonds set in platinum. I had been so intent on Mrs. Jones' distress that I hadn't noticed the missing rings. "Let me check her room," I said. I rushed from the dining room and back to Mrs. Jones' room. Jean was standing at the nurses' station as I passed.

"Nora, what's wrong?" she asked.

"Mrs. Jones' rings are missing!" I exclaimed. At the room, I paused in the doorway. It was a private room, sunny yellow with frilly white curtains and old pine furniture. Everything belonged to Mrs. Jones. I looked around the room, trying to absorb every detail. Where could the rings be?

Jean was behind me. "Did you check the drawers?" she asked.

"I didn't check anything yet," I replied. "Her daughter just discovered they were missing."

"You check the drawers and the closet," said Jean. "I'll check the bed."

Twenty minutes later, nothing. Jean and I were still searching as Lonnie wheeled Mrs. Jones back into the room. Tanya McCluskey was with them. "Any luck?" she asked.

"Not yet," Jean replied.

"Then you folks have a problem," said Mrs. McCluskey. "I want to see the Claytons!"

Chapter 2

"We'll have to talk with everyone on staff," said Jacobsport police detective Dan Maguire. He stood at the nurses' station with Sam Clayton, the owner and administrator of Marian Manor. I was standing with Jean, across the counter from the men.

Detective Maguire was not much older than me. With medium height and build, medium brown hair and hazel eyes, he had that "All-American" face that now looked quite serious as he studied his surroundings. I wondered if being "average" was an important part of being a detective.

"That's fine with us," said Sam. "We want to know what happened to the rings. Maybe they just slipped off her finger?" He tilted his head and raised his eyebrows, looking over at Jean. Sam was short and chubby, with thinning red hair and a smiling, freckled face.

Marian Manor was named for Sam's mother, Marian, a nurse who had been devoted to caring for the elderly in Jacobsport. How the staff treated residents was important to Sam. Either he or his wife Iris visited each unit daily to be sure all was well.

"I'd like to talk with Mrs. Jones' daughter first, if you don't mind," said Detective Maguire as he walked back towards Room

219. We had taken Mrs. Jones back to her room for breakfast, so as not to upset the other residents in the dining room.

"I just can't believe this, Sam," said Jean after Detective Maguire left. Her eyes were following the detective down the hallway as she stood wringing her hands. Sam was pacing in front of the desk.

"I'm sure there will be a simple explanation," said Sam. "We'll wonder why we didn't think of it sooner."

"I hope so," said Jean, "but this isn't the only odd thing that's happened today."

"What do you mean?" Sam asked.

"Well, you know Harriet Allen passed away last night," said Jean.

"I know," Sam replied. "She'll be missed."

"When I went to see her," Jean began, "I found her call light on the floor behind the head of the bed."

"What's odd about that?" Sam asked. "It probably dropped sometime after she died, when they were checking her."

"Perhaps," said Jean, "but her watch was in the bedside stand."

"That is odd," I said. "Harriet loved that watch."

"I don't follow," said Sam.

"The watch glowed in the dark and had big numbers so she could see them," I replied. "The staff made sure she had it on at all times because of her poor eyesight. It's very odd that she wasn't wearing it."

"What are you suggesting?" Sam asked.

"I'm not sure," I said.

"I didn't think much about it at the time," said Jean, but I think I'll check on her jewelry. See if anything is missing." She started down the hall like a torpedo after a target.

"Just remember," Sam called after her, "we have 159 other residents who still need our care." He said this last part as he set off down the hall towards the stairwell.

I knew Sam was right, but it was going to be hard concentrating on my work with all this excitement. It was now 9:00 and I hadn't even started the morning medicines.

Some mornings I may prepare over two hundred meds for my team of twenty residents. Sometimes these meds have to be crushed and mixed with applesauce or pudding so that the resident can swallow the med. There are also wound dressings to change and breathing treatments to give. And I liked having time to talk with the residents too. That's the best part of being a nurse—or almost a nurse.

As I was outlining my plan for the day, I heard a voice behind me, "Miss Brady?"

"Yes," I replied, turning around. It was Detective Maguire.

"Do you have time for a few questions?" he asked.

I really didn't, but given the looks of my schedule, there would be no good time. "Sure, if it doesn't take too long," I said. "I'm kind of behind this morning."

"It shouldn't take too long," he said. "There are just a few questions. Maybe you can tell me about Mrs. Jones. I understand you're the nurse who generally cares for her during the day."

"Nursing student," I corrected.

"O.K., nursing student," he replied, like "What's the difference?"

I had to think quickly. I wanted to answer the detective's questions, but I had to be careful about a resident's privacy. "We can use Jean's office," I said as I led him through the nurses' station into the office. I indicated Jean's chair behind her desk, or the little table and chairs Jean had off to one side. He chose the table. I liked that. It was less intimidating.

"So, how long have you worked here, Miss Brady? Or may I call you Nora?" he asked, flipping through a small notebook.

"Nora is fine," I replied, wondering if I was being professional. Being "professional" was constantly emphasized in my classes.

"About a month."

"A month?" he questioned.

"That I've worked here," I replied. "Only I don't really work here. I'm a student. I don't get paid."

Detective Maguire looked confused. "Well, how do you like it here?"

"I like it," I said. "Jean, our manager, is a really good nurse and I'm learning a lot. There are a lot of nice people and I love the residents, or most of them, anyway."

"Most of them?" he asked.

"Well, you know," I replied, "there are always a few that aren't so easy to get along with."

"Mrs. Jones?" he asked.

"Oh no! Mrs. Jones is really sweet," I said. It's been hard for her after the strokes. Sometimes it's difficult to know what she wants or needs, but I love taking care of her. She's one of my favorites."

"Has anyone else ever reported anything missing?" he asked.

"Well, probably everyone up here, who is here for awhile, has things missing from time to time, but we usually find them," I explained. "It's usually clothing that accidentally goes into the laundry, or someone's glasses or teeth that go to the kitchen with a returned meal tray."

"What about any missing jewelry? A watch? Earrings? Maybe even a radio or small TV? Try to remember," he said. He got up from the table, crossed his arms and started pacing the small office. "It's important."

"I don't remember anyone else losing anything, but I'll think about it," I said, wondering what he knew that I didn't. "Maybe you need to talk with the staff that's here all the time."

"Don't worry. We'll be talking to everyone," said Detective Maguire, sounding somewhat annoyed. He reached into his pocket and then handed me his card. "If you think of anything, please call me. The smallest thing could be useful." I got up from my chair and walked to the door. "Thanks for your time," he said, extending his hand. "Would you please ask Tina Kunz to step in?" I shook his hand, but just as I started out the door, he suddenly asked: "Did you ever take care of Harriet Allen? On 2 East?"

"Yes," I replied, startled by his change of direction. "Why?"

"What can you tell me about her?" he asked, not answering my question.

"I didn't know her very well, but I liked her," I replied. "She was a bright lady with a nice family. I was sorry to hear she died." I studied Detective Maguire's face, but I couldn't tell what he was thinking.

"Well, thanks again," he said. I was being dismissed. Why had he asked about Harriet Allen? Did Jean have a reason to be suspicious?

I found Tina for Detective Maguire and then I got started on my assignment. The rest of the day was extremely busy. Tanya McCluskey had gone back to work and Mrs. Jones was calm and smiling when I gave her meds. All the assigned baths and beds were done by lunchtime. I guessed that Dominic had helped Lonnie.

At the end of our shift, Tina and I sat across from each other in the conference room. We were finishing our charts, and, as there were no computers, we wrote everything by hand. I don't know who said it, but a nurse learns very quickly that, in healthcare: "If it's not written, it's not been done."

"So how was your talk with Detective Maguire?" I asked Tina.

"O.K., I guess," Tina replied. "I really couldn't be of much help. I never took care of Mrs. Jones and I couldn't remember any other theft."

"Do you really think anyone would steal from these defenseless people?" I asked.

"Those are the best kind," laughed Tina. "You really are too naïve, Nora."

"And you are too cynical, Tina," I paused. "O.K., just say there was someone who did steal, who could that be?"

"I don't know," said Tina. "If I had to pick someone, I would probably pick Lonnie."

"Why's that?" I asked.

"I don't trust her," said Tina. "I've found her rummaging in some of the rooms and I think she's sneaky. I don't know how they work with her everyday."

"I know exactly what you mean," I said. "I find the same thing. But wouldn't there be other signs? Like buying stuff she couldn't afford? I haven't seen any of that with Lonnie."

"You're right," said Tina.

"I wonder what Jean thinks?" I said.

As if on cue, Jean's head appeared in the doorway. "Are you two almost finished with those charts? The evening crew is going to need them soon and you two need to get home."

"Jean, do you have a few minutes?" I asked.

"It's been a long day, Nora," said Jean. Her eyelids were sagging.

"We've been trying to figure out who might have taken those rings," said Tina.

Jean gave us a long, hard look. She wasn't one to hurry when making a decision, or when asked for her opinion. She was a fast worker and a slow talker who never asked the staff to do something she wouldn't do herself. The staff liked her. "We don't know that anyone took the rings," she replied.

"But …," I started to say.

"But nothing," said Jean. "Now is not the time to be accusing anyone."

"We were wondering what you thought about Lonnie," ventured Tina.

"I understand your need for answers," said Jean, "but I think you're barking up the wrong tree. Lonnie is slow—thinking and working. I know that. And, yes, she has to do things her own way, but she really is a good person and I don't believe that she's a thief." She paused. "Let's hope that this is all a big misunderstanding. Just maybe those rings slipped off Melba's finger and got lost in the laundry, like Sam said."

"But Mrs. McCluskey said the rings had just been sized so that wouldn't happen," I said.

"Would you just let me dream for awhile, Nora?" Jean asked this as she gave us a final nod and started to close the conference room door.

"Wait, Jean," I called. "Did you find anything missing from Harriet Allen's things?"

"Not that I could tell," she replied. "I'm waiting for the family to go through things." Then, without waiting for my response, she closed the door.

"So what did you think about Detective Maguire?" asked Tina, resuming our conversation.

"I really don't know," I replied. "He seemed nice enough, but kind of young."

Tina is always trying to match people up. Any available guy is a match either for herself or for one of her friends. Her latest boyfriend was someone who stopped to help her with a flat tire. Then he had a friend that Tina fixed up with someone who worked in the kitchen at Marian Manor.

"Jean told me she grew up with Dan's mother, but then the family moved to Sacramento. Jean hasn't seen them in years. Dan's not much older than us," said Tina. "I guess his father is also a policeman," Tina continued. "He was shot during a robbery or something and he's in a wheelchair, but he still works. Jean says that Dan moved up here to be close to the water. He's the outdoors type." Trust Tina to get the details.

"Well, I just hope he's a good detective," I said. "These residents need to feel safe."

"I agree," said Tina.

"Did he say anything to you about Harriet Allen?" I asked.

"No, why would he?" asked Tina.

"I don't know," I replied, "but he asked me about her."

We looked at each other a moment. Then, shrugging our shoulders, we went back to working on the charts. After work, I ran some errands before going home. By the time I did get home, I was exhausted. I had to study, but I also wanted some time to think about what had happened. Was there a thief? And what did all this have to do with Harriet Allen?

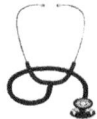

Chapter 3

I knew something was wrong as soon as I walked into the nurses' station the next morning. Jean was sitting at the desk and she looked grim. The rest of the staff was quiet. Before I could ask what was wrong, Ruth Rice began her report.

"I have some bad news," she said. "Melba Jones passed away last night." There was a catch in Ruth's voice. "Everything was fine when we came on. She even smiled at me on my first few rounds. When I checked on her at 2:00, she wasn't breathing."

"Did you call 911?" I asked.

Jean placed her hand on my arm. "You know Melba didn't want any CPR, Nora." I nodded, remembering. I felt dizzy. Everything seemed to be happening too quickly.

"Tanya and her husband came in," Ruth continued. "That wasn't pretty. She was screaming that we had murdered her mother. She had everyone upset. The husband tried to calm her down, but she just wasn't ready for her mother to pass."

"She was probably even more upset after what happened yesterday," said Jean.

"I heard about that," said Ruth. "We're waiting for the coroner now."

"What has this got to do with the coroner?" I questioned. "No one can seriously think anyone here would harm Melba!" The coroner was only called when there were suspicious circumstances surrounding a death, or if someone died within 24 hours of coming into a hospital or nursing home.

"Apparently her daughter does think it's possible," said Jean.

"Just the thought of that makes me sick," I said, getting up. I needed a few moments alone. The dining room was close, but I didn't want to see any residents just yet. I started walking towards the conference room.

As I pushed open the door to the conference room, I realized, too late, that there were voices on the other side. It was Tanya McCluskey talking with Detective Maguire. "I'm sorry," I said. "I didn't realize anyone was in here. I'm so sorry to hear about your mother, Mrs. McCluskey." I wondered where Mr. McCluskey had gone.

Tanya McCluskey's face was tear streaked and her mascara was smudged on the lower lids. She was dressed in baggy, black sweats and had obviously come here in a hurry. She didn't respond. Detective Maguire looked tired. He also looked like he had dressed in a hurry, wearing worn jeans and a faded T-shirt under some kind of a team jacket. I briefly wondered what kind of sport he played.

"We're going to be here for a while, Nora," said Detective Maguire.

"Of course," I said. "I'm sorry." I closed the door, paused and leaned back against the wall. Then I bent over and drew a few deep breaths. Straightening up, I headed back to the nurses' station. Tina was coming towards me.

"Are you all right?" she asked. "I was just coming to find you."

"I'm fine," I said. "Just shocked. Tanya McCluskey is with Detective Maguire in the conference room. I hoped to have a few minutes to myself, but no such luck."

"I know you really cared about Mrs. Jones," said Tina, "but she was getting up there. I'm sure she died of natural causes. Ruth said that Dr. McCain is coming in early and there will likely be some special examination of the body to determine the cause of death."

"An autopsy!" I exclaimed. "I was supposed to talk with Dr. McCain yesterday. About Melba. In all the excitement I forgot to call him. Maybe he could have done something for her."

"Well, here he comes now with Sam," said Tina.

Sam Clayton and Dr. McCain were walking towards us. Dr. McCain was both our medical director and Melba Jones' doctor. The two men looked to be deep in conversation. Then, coming behind them was Jimmy Ramirez, the assistant coroner and a friend of mine. I liked Jimmy and it had nothing to do with his good looks. He was a few years ahead of me in school and we had dated a few times, but then decided we were better as friends. He now dated my friend Erin Farley.

We watched Sam motion the men into the conference room. I was full of questions. Going back to the unit was the last thing I wanted to do, but Jean was calling us.

My assignment was much the same as yesterday, except that my team was smaller since Deborah was back. It seemed that Deborah was sick a lot. I looked over at her. She didn't look sick, but she never looked particularly well either. She was pretty, but skinny and pale with long blond hair that was lank and lifeless. When she walked over to ask some question of Tina, I noted the contrast. It was like comparing a mushroom with a fresh picked apple. Deborah is about five years older than Tina and me, but this morning, she looked old enough to be our mother. "Maybe she really is sick!" I thought, but then I caught myself. Nurses have a tendency to diagnose everyone.

As I started to set up my med cart, I noticed Mr. Jessel and Mr. Parker entering the dining room. I poured and delivered their whiskeys first. I was running late again, but since I was working with Dominic today, I didn't have to worry about helping any residents up for breakfast.

Next, I checked blood sugars on the two diabetic residents on my team and then prepared their insulin injections. I started passing the morning meds, trying to spend a few moments chatting with each resident. As I guided my cart down the hall, I saw Detective Maguire leave Melba Jones' room. Tanya McCluskey and Jimmy Ramirez were with him. I guessed they were ready to transport the body to the morgue at the county coroner's office.

I saw Dr. McCain sitting at the nurses' station, writing in a chart. Short, thin and stooped, with a graying flat top and heavy black-rimmed glasses, he looked almost as old as his patients. I liked him because he always listened to my concerns and treated me like I had a brain in my head. He treated nurses like part of the team, unlike some of the other doctors, who act as if nurses, especially student nurses, were little more than servants. "What did you all decide about Mrs. Jones?" I asked him.

"There will be an autopsy," he replied, in his decidedly southern drawl. "I'm leaving the details up to Detective Maguire and Mr. Ramirez."

"I meant to talk with you yesterday," I said. "We were worried about Mrs. Jones, but couldn't quite figure out what the problem was. And then you probably heard about the missing rings? It had everyone upset. It's hard to believe that anyone would steal from a resident. In all the turmoil, I forgot to call you." I was rambling.

Dr. McCain looked up at me and leaned back in his chair. "Actually I did see Melba yesterday," he said. "Jean called me on something else and mentioned the nurses' concerns. You must have been tied up in another room when I came by. I couldn't find anything different. Her agitation about the rings had subsided by the time I saw her and her blood pressure was fine. We did draw some blood and you can see the results here are all within normal limits." He handed me the chart, opened to the lab reports. "With her long history of strokes, I think it's just a coincidence that she passed away at this time. Nonetheless, we have to be sure."

When I finished talking with Dr. McCain, I turned to find Jimmy standing at the nurses' station counter. "Hey Nora, how are you?" he asked. "Haven't seen you in a while. How's your golf game?"

"Haven't had much time lately, Jimmy," I replied. Jimmy and I had taken an introductory course together. We both liked golf a lot, but Jimmy was a fanatic. As it turned out, my friend Erin was an excellent golfer, which was one of the reasons they had hit it off.

"What are you doing Saturday morning?" he asked. "Erin and I were thinking of getting together a foursome. Are you free?"

"I have to work this weekend and I have a big test to study for," I said, "but maybe we can all have dinner one night?"

"Sounds good to me," Jimmy replied. "Any particular night? I'm usually tied up at work until about 7:00. And I'm usually on call Thursdays and Fridays, so I'd have to be available to come into work if I'm needed.

"I can work around your schedule," I said. "I'll give Erin a call."

As we finished talking, Detective Maguire, who seemed to have been freed from Tanya McCluskey, joined Jimmy. "Hey Dan, you're a golfer, aren't you?" Jimmy asked, patting him on the back.

"Not since high school," laughed Detective Maguire. "I've been thinking of taking it up again. Just haven't made the time."

"Well, you're in luck," said Jimmy. "We were just talking about getting together a foursome. Nora and I took our first class together and we haven't played together in a long time."

Detective Maguire's eyes flicked quickly between Jimmy and me. I could see the hesitation. "I doubt if I'm in your league," he said, "but maybe one of these days. Is there anything more you need, Jimmy? I've got to get back to the station." His tone was professional.

"I don't think so, Dan. We'll be in touch," said Jimmy. "If you want to wait a second, I'll walk out with you. I just have to get my clipboard." Jimmy stepped back into Melba Jones' room. Two men from the coroner's office were in the room and had just finished placing Melba Jones' body onto the gurney for transfer to the morgue. Jimmy spoke to them briefly and then stepped back into the hall. He called a quick goodbye to me and joined Detective Maguire, already halfway down the hall. The men with the gurney followed.

I was somewhat annoyed with Jimmy. He had put both Detective Maguire and me on the spot. It looked like we were being set up and I didn't like that. Apparently, neither did Detective Maguire.

It was a busy morning and by lunchtime, I had put the conversation with Jimmy completely out of my mind. On my way back from lunch, I stopped in the Activities department. I knew Kathy, the Activities Director, and Mr. Parker would be busy working at the computer. I was curious as to how they were doing.

Kathy had been introducing Mr. Parker to the Internet so he could explore his family history. He knew he had been adopted, but no one talked about adoptions when he was growing up. "It just never ceases to amaze me," said Mr. Parker, "how much you can learn from this Internet. It's just wonderful."

"We haven't had much luck with government records," said Kathy, "so we're going to try the newspapers. We'll research the newspaper records using Mr. Parker's birth date. If the information isn't online, we'll write to the newspaper. If Mr. Parker was adopted, it's likely that his parents lived in this area."

"It wasn't unusual for a family to give up a child for adoption," said Mr. Parker, "if there were too many mouths to feed and another family really wanted a child." He was staring intently at the monitor and I left them to their work.

I had plenty to keep me busy for the remainder of the day. I still had some afternoon meds and, of course, I had to finish my charting. Once a week, we have to write a brief summary on how each resident is doing with things like eating, walking, bathroom habits, and skin. Today was the day.

I sat down at the nurses' station, and started pulling charts. I thought I had just enough time to finish the charts, before I had to give the afternoon meds. Dominic and Tara were passing afternoon snacks and filling the residents' pitchers with fresh ice water. I didn't see Lonnie. I didn't see any of the nurses either, but I thought they might be doing treatments or answering call lights. Tina had gone to a late lunch.

Jean was in her office and I heard her call out for Deborah. I got up and walked over to the office door. "She isn't out here, Jean," I said, "but I'll go find her, if you want."

"Thank you," said Jean.

I walked down towards Deborah's end of the hall. As I walked past room 205, I saw the blur of someone moving in the room. It didn't register with me at first, but when I stepped back, I realized it was Deborah. She was bent over the bedside table by the second bed, rooting around in the top drawer. She didn't see me standing there as she withdrew something from the drawer and quickly slipped it into her pocket. Like all of us, Deborah wore scrubs with lots of pockets—pockets on the legs, pockets in the tops, and pockets in the jackets. Nurses need lots of pockets so they can carry lots of different things, so they're prepared to deal with anything!

"Deborah," I said from the doorway. "Jean is looking for you. What's up? Did Mrs. Michaels lose something?"

"No," said Deborah. "I think she's been hiding food in these drawers again and I don't want a repeat of the ant problem. What does Jean want?" she asked. As Deborah was talking, her eyes roamed the room. She didn't look at me.

"I didn't ask her," I said. "I just said I'd find you."

We walked back to the nurses' station together. I was bothered by what I had seen, but I was trying not to jump to conclusions. Still, what had Deborah put in her pocket?

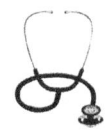

Chapter 4

Death is expected in a nursing home, but I felt bad when it seemed we forgot people so soon. Life goes on. A new resident had been admitted into Melba Jones' room. His name was Isaac Lowenstein, a short, wiry and talkative gentleman. He seemed to get along particularly well with Mr. Parker and Mr. Jessel. The three men discovered they had friends in common and had belonged to some of the same clubs. Mr. Parker and Mr. Jessel had lived in San Francisco and Mr. Lowenstein had moved up from there as his nephew lived in Jacobsport. Dominic and I had the team that included these three men and Dominic enjoyed them as much as I did.

Dominic looked like a 49ers halfback. He had even thought about playing professional football, but then he severely damaged one of his legs in a car accident. School was never important to Dominic before the accident. Now he was working at Marian Manor to save money for college and he hoped to one day teach and coach sports. We were encouraging him to consider nursing. Nursing needs more men.

The residents loved talking sports with Dominic. He would be missed when he left for college. The staff would also miss him as Dominic was one of those people who got along with everyone. Some of us thought Tara had a crush on Dominic, but neither of these two ever said anything. Once, I found a yellow rose sitting on top of Tara's jacket and books in the break room, but she wouldn't tell me where it had come from. She just smiled.

Tara was a different kettle of fish. Tall and slender, with long, curly red hair, she was shy with staff, but with a resident, she could talk non-stop. She could also sing. Sometimes we would find her singing softly while bathing a resident. Other times, when she thought she was alone, we might find her belting out some song while making a bed. It was beautiful. Tara hoped to become a nurse, but she wanted to work first to decide if she really liked it. Tina and Tara made a good team as Tina liked to talk and Tara liked to listen.

It was less than a week after Melba Jones' death. I was at the nurses' station going over a chart. The day was going to be busy. Dr. McCain was doing his "rounds," seeing all his patients. That meant Jean would be tied up and then the nurses would have a stack of paperwork to review. It wasn't my kind of day. Like most nurses, I preferred to be doing almost anything other than paperwork.

"Nora, could I see you for a minute, please?" Jean was standing at the door to her office.

Tina, who was sitting across from me, looked up and smiled. "Now what did you do?" she teased.

"Nothing," I said, a little defensively. "Like you're one to talk." I got up and walked to the office.

"Have a seat," said Jean. "This will only take a moment. I just wanted to see if you might like to try doing rounds with Dr. McCain today. I have some paperwork to catch up on and it looks like your assignment is under control. I think it would be good experience for you and Tina. It's on the checklist from Mrs. Floyd, your instructor.

"I would love to make rounds," I said. "There's so much to learn from the doctors and most of the time we don't have them around for questions. What do I have to do?"

"Just give Dr. McCain an update on each resident's condition and review the current doctor's orders," said Jean. "Check to see if the resident still needs everything that's ordered, or if there are some new orders we need. Pay particular attention to the meds. Then check with the nurse who's assigned to the resident to see if there's anything new or anything she wants. How does that sound?" Nurses must have a doctor's order for everything they do for a patient.

"Great!" I said.

"You know, Nora, you've got me thinking," said Jean. "There's a lot a nurse can learn by doing rounds with the doctor. Perhaps I should have each nurse doing rounds on her own team. They could give the doctor a better picture of how a resident is doing and bring up any concerns. You students are always giving me ideas!"

"I'm glad we're doing something for you, Jean," I said. "We appreciate everything you do for us. We know students take a lot of time."

"Well, let's see how it goes for you all and Dr. McCain today," said Jean. "If it works, I'll run it past Mrs. Dixon, our Director of Nursing, at our next managers' meeting. Maybe we'll want to have all the nurses at Marian Manor doing this. We want nurses to have control over their work and to feel a real part of the team!"

There was a knock at the door, and Tina's head appeared. "Dr. McCain is here, Jean."

"Maybe I should talk with him for a minute before we try this, Nora," said Jean, "just to see what he thinks."

"About what?" asked Dr. McCain, appearing in the doorway, behind Tina.

Jean explained the new plan. Dr. McCain nodded along, as she was speaking. "Sounds good to me," he said.

"Sounds wonderful to me," said Tina. "I'd love to try it."

"Then I guess I'm the first to go with you," I said turning to Dr. McCain.

"I'll talk with the other nurses," said Jean.

I left and began collecting my charts and placing them on the little cart that we used for making rounds. I also collected the supplies that I knew Jean always brought along: gloves, betadine, Q-tips, tongue blades, the opthalmascope for examining eyes and the otoscope for examining ears.

It took about two hours to see all of the residents on my team and then Dr. McCain went on to see other residents, stopping only for lunch. I learned a lot watching Dr. McCain examine the residents and he took time to explain things to me.

When I was little, I wanted to be a nurse just like my mother. As I got older, it seemed to me that a nurse was just a doctor's assistant, so I wanted to be a doctor. Then, two summers ago, when I couldn't get a job anywhere else, I started working as an aide at the hospital. I saw things differently. Nurses had to be smart. They could go anywhere in the world, work in all kinds of places, teach or manage or do research and wear really comfortable clothes. And, patients made them feel good. I wanted to be part of all that.

As I sat at the desk at the end of the day, thinking about my rounds with Dr. McCain and what I liked about nursing, I heard Dr. McCain talking with Jean in her office. They made no attempt to close the door or to whisper, so I didn't feel the need to move away. I didn't hear everything, but it was obvious that Dr. McCain was not happy.

"She doesn't know her team," said Dr. McCain. "I don't know how else to say it. She couldn't tell me blood pressures, or how any wounds were progressing. She didn't know how well people were sleeping or how often they used their pain meds."

"Well, she's been sick a lot lately," said Jean. "Maybe that's why she's not up on some of this. But she should know what happened today. I'll talk with her."

"There was a big difference between the reports I got from the students and the one I got from Deborah," said Dr. McCain. "Maybe she's no longer interested in this kind of work. It's not fair to the residents to have someone working with them, who doesn't like the work."

"I'll talk with her," Jean repeated. "Maybe she's still not well and I just haven't given her enough attention. Is there anything else? Any big changes in anyone that I should know about?"

"No, everything else is fine," said Dr. McCain. "You're doing a great job, Jean. Thanks for listening."

I sat back in my chair and thought about what I had heard. Dr. McCain was right. Something was going on with Deborah. Again, I thought about what I had seen several days ago, about Deborah rooting around in Mrs. Michael's drawer.

Deborah had said she was afraid that Mrs. Michaels was hoarding food and that she didn't want to see any more ants in there. But did Mrs. Michaels really hoard food? And what was it that Deborah had put in her pocket? What did I really know about this nurse? Why was she sick all the time? Did she have any friends? I hated to even think about it, but was her behavior in any way related to the thefts or to the sudden death of Melba Jones? I had to learn more about Deborah.

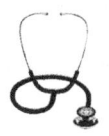

Chapter 5

The next day, Deborah was absent again. I was disappointed and it must have showed. As I sat at the nurses' station, reviewing care plans and preparing my schedule, Tina rolled her chair up beside me. "What's with you today?" she asked.

"What do you mean?" I said.

"You look kind of depressed," she replied.

"Well, I had this big plan." I paused, waiting for Tina's reaction ... some snide comment about my previous schemes.

Tina said nothing.

"I want to know more about Deborah," I ventured. "I was going to try and talk with her and here she calls in sick again."

"What's the deal?" asked Tina. "I mean, why is knowing about Deborah important?"

"I don't know," I said. "Maybe I could learn something from her." I really didn't want to discuss my suspicions with Tina. It wouldn't be fair, especially if I was wrong.

"Well, I'm not crazy about Deborah," said Tina. "She's not very friendly and she's made it clear that she thinks students are pond scum."

"Do you know anything about her?" I asked. Tina always had the scoop on everyone.

"Only that she moved here from San Francisco," Tina replied. "I don't know why she picked Jacobsport, or if she worked anywhere else in this area before coming to Marian Manor. I don't know if she dates anyone, or if she plays any sports. I've never heard her talk about anything outside of work, but I haven't tried very hard to know her."

"Can you help me?" I asked.

"If you think it's important," said Tina.

"What are you two up to?" asked Jean coming up behind us.

"We were just saying that we don't know Deborah very well," I replied. "We're going to make more of an effort."

"That's a great idea!" said Jean. "Maybe part of Deborah's frequent illnesses is just loneliness."

"Do you know what Deborah likes to do, or why she's here in Jacobsport?" I asked.

"I think you need to ask her those questions yourself, Nora," said Jean. "Now isn't it time for you two to be out on the unit? We don't want Lisa thinking that things have slacked off around here." Lisa Duncan was another RN working with us today. She had been the nurse manager before Jean, but had left to start a family.

Tina and I finished our schedules and started towards our med carts. As I glanced down the hall, I saw Detective Maguire enter from the stairwell.

"Good morning," I said. Tina echoed my greeting. "Anything new on the Melba Jones case?" I asked.

"No, I'm sorry," said Detective Maguire. "I'm here about another theft. I just came from talking with Mr. and Mrs. Clayton."

"Another theft?" Tina and I silently mouthed. "Who? What? When? Why?" we asked at the same time.

"I really can't give you the specifics at this time, but I'll need to speak with everyone on staff again," he replied. "Is Jean here? I'll check with her first."

Detective Maguire walked towards Jean's office. Tina and I stared after him.

"I can't believe this," I said.

"You and me, both," said Tina.

"What are we going to do?" I asked. "This gives you second thoughts about everyone."

"I know," said Tina, "but we can't be jumping to conclusions."

"That's very mature of you," I said.

Tina gave me a prissy smile as we started setting up our carts. We didn't talk for several minutes, but my mind was racing. "Have you noticed that every time something shows up missing, Deborah is off sick?" I asked.

"Don't go there, Nora," said Tina. "There could be lots of reasons for that. You were just talking about needing to know her better."

"You're right, Tina," I said. "I'm looking at the obvious and it's unfair. We could apply the nursing process to figure this out, you know. Identify the problem. Consider all possible explanations. Test the possibilities. Evaluate the results."

"Or ...," said Tina. "We could just let the police do their job and we could do ours."

"When did you get to be so levelheaded?" I asked with a laugh.

Tina smiled. "The same time you morphed into Nancy Drew. See you later." She pushed her cart into the hall, leaving me to my thoughts.

The morning went quickly and soon I found myself helping residents down to lunch. I was walking with Mr. Skinner, a tall, frail man who was still somewhat weak from a recent cold. Even with a flannel shirt and two layers of sweaters, I could feel his bony elbow on my arm. I had really pushed him to come down to the dining room.

Mrs. Danner and Mrs. Michaels were walking ahead of us

and they were deep in conversation. Mrs. Michaels seemed rather agitated, her white curls shaking from side to side as she talked. She had a tendency to over-react to things. Like the time she found those ants in her bedside table. Her screams brought staff from every area of the building. You would have thought an axe murderer was attacking her. It took hours to calm her down. I often wondered if she had ever considered being an actress.

"The detective told me not to say anything, but I just have to tell you," said Mrs. Michaels, a little too loudly. People with poor hearing often speak louder than necessary. "I wouldn't want this to happen to you too," she continued. "My family says I should think about moving someplace else, but I don't want to leave all my friends here."

"It was only a letter opener, June," said Mrs. Danner. Charlotte Danner was the perfect friend for June Michaels. Nothing seemed to ruffle Mrs. Danner, but that wasn't exactly true. She was always willing to listen to someone's problems and she readily shared her own. She saw problems everywhere, from her family to the soup at dinnertime. The one thing she didn't have problems with was her hair. She was envied by many of the residents for her thick dark hair, natural at 80. The staff's only concern was that she spent too much time alone, often dwelling on her problems, or those of her friends.

"It was a solid silver letter opener, Charlotte, and it's been in my family for years," said Mrs. Michaels. "My mother gave it to me when I got married. I couldn't even bear parting with it when my own children got married. That's why I still have it … had it."

"Well, why aren't you supposed to say anything, June?" asked Mrs. Danner.

"They don't want anyone to have too many details, I guess," Mrs. Michaels replied. "I really don't know why. Mrs. Clayton came up to see me, personally, and she was very upset. She's so nice. She stops in to see me almost every week. She promised to give this her full attention."

"I know," said Mrs. Danner. "Mrs. Clayton is very nice. She comes in to talk with me almost every week, too. I call her *Iris*."

"I call her Iris, too," said Mrs. Michaels huffily. "I just wasn't sure that you'd know who I meant." The two ladies continued into the dining room.

"This may explain Detective Maguire's visit," I thought to myself, as I helped Mr. Skinner into his dining room chair.

"Thank you, dear," said Mr. Skinner. "You're always so patient with me. You never try to rush me when we walk. I really appreciate that."

"You're very welcome, Mr. Skinner," I said. "I'm just glad to see you getting up again. Staying in bed too much isn't good for you. We have to keep that blood moving and build up those muscles."

Mr. Skinner laughed and held up a scrawny arm in an attempt to show me his muscle. I laughed and walked away feeling a bit guilty. I had walked slowly with Mr. Skinner, but not just because he was weak. I wanted to hear the conversation that Mrs. Michaels was having with Mrs. Danner.

Detective Maguire had been meeting with staff all morning. I guessed that my turn was coming up pretty soon. No sooner had the thought passed through my mind than Jean called to me from the nurses' station.

"Nora, do you have a few minutes," she asked.

"Sure. I'll be there in a second," I answered. Luckily I was caught up.

"Detective Maguire is using my office again to talk with the staff," said Jean. "It shouldn't take too long."

Detective Maguire was sitting behind Jean's desk this time and he appeared to be quite at home. "Have a seat, Nora," he said. "I'm asking each of the staff the same questions. If you can answer them, fine. If you don't have any answer, just say so. O.K.?"

"I'll help in any way I can," I said.

"Good," he said. "First off, I can't tell you much, but what was taken is of considerable value."

"I think I know what this is about," I said. "I overheard Mrs. Michaels talking with Mrs. Danner this morning. It sounds as if there was a silver letter opener taken."

"That's right," he answered. "But it's more than that. There was also a pearl necklace, with a diamond clasp. I'd appreciate it if you'd keep that to yourself," he added quickly, looking a little flushed. "Mrs. Michaels was particularly attached to the letter opener. Do you have any idea what might have happened?"

I hesitated and thought of Deborah rooting around in Mrs. Michaels' drawer. Was it really a question of ants? "No, I don't know what happened, or why, or who might have taken the items," I replied. I couldn't accuse Deborah without some proof. What had she put in her pocket?

"What can you tell me about Deborah Cullen?" asked Detective Maguire.

"I can't tell you much," I said, wondering if he could read minds. "She doesn't talk much to students." I paused. "There isn't much time to get to know people at work, unless you're working directly with them. Nurses usually work more with the aides than with each other. Deborah seems to get her work done. She doesn't argue with anyone that I know of."

"How about Lonnie Simpson?" he continued.

"Well, Lonnie usually works with Deborah," I said. "Occasionally I work with Lonnie, but I don't really know her very well either. We have some problems working together."

"Problems?" asked Detective Maguire.

"Lonnie and I don't work at the same pace," I explained. "I think she's a bit slow and she doesn't always give the care I think should be given. Also, she doesn't take direction very well and she tends to fly off the handle easily. I just find her difficult to work with." As an afterthought, I added, "I don't know anything about her personal life."

"And what do you know about Dominic Angelini?" he continued.

"I love working with Dominic," I said. "He really cares about the residents and goes out of his way to do the little things for them. He's saving money for college and I think he wants to be a teacher. I paused. "I don't know much about his personal life. I know he plays some soccer and football. He does talk about that, but that's about it."

"You certainly have some very definite ideas about people. Guess I'd better stay on your good side," laughed Detective Maguire.

He asked similar questions about the remaining staff, including Jean. Then surprisingly he asked, "What about one of the other residents taking the jewelry?"

"I suppose anything is possible," I replied, "but I really can't see it. No one seems to need money. Why else would someone steal?"

"What about a resident stealing just for the thrill of it?" he countered. "What about kleptomania, stealing because of an illness?"

"I don't think the thief would target only the most valuable articles, if mental illness was involved," I replied. "I think people like that will take anything, but I don't know. I haven't done my psych rotation yet. Have you talked with Dr. McCain?"

"Dr. McCain agrees with you," said Detective Maguire. "I just wanted another take on the situation. You seem to be objective." He paused, checking his notes. "I think that's all for now," he said. "Would you please send in Tina?" I was being dismissed. "And thanks again for your input," he added.

We finished the day without further excitement, but my conversation with Detective Maguire had again given me food for thought. I realized how little I knew most of the staff, not just Deborah. And what about the residents? Could one of them be the thief?

Chapter 6

When I got home that evening, my landlady, Stella Margoles, was waiting by her front door, looking very worried. She was tiny, white haired, elegant and nearing her 90th birthday. Listening to her stories, I thought she had been everywhere, knew everyone and done everything. Nothing could surprise her or disturb her calm. "What's the matter, Stella?" I asked. "You look upset."

"Oh Nora, it's been a terrible day," said Stella. "First, I couldn't find Eugene." Eugene was Stella's ancient Siamese cat, named for Eugene O'Neill. The playwright had been a great friend of Stella's in her younger days. "Then the water heater in your apartment broke and water started seeping through my ceiling. I'm so sorry. The plumbers are up there now, but your carpet is soaked and my ceiling is going to need major repairs, which means your floor will probably have to be replaced." By now, Stella was crying. This wasn't like her.

"Don't worry, Stella," I said. "It can all be fixed. I'm not home that much anyway." I put my arms around her thin shoulders.

"But I'm not sure you can stay in your apartment," said Stella. "It may not be safe. There may not be any running water. I'm so sorry. I'd say move in with me, but there isn't much room, considering all the junk I have."

"Don't worry, Stella," I said again. "I'll stay with a friend."

"It could be several weeks, Nora," she said. "I knew I should have cleaned out those back bedrooms. I'm so sorry." She was still crying.

"That's O.K. I can stay with friends." I reassured her, searching my pockets. "Do you mind if I use your phone to call my friend Tina?" I asked. "I must have left my cell in the car."

"Anything you want, Nora," she said.

I walked through the front door and paused in the foyer, not sure which way to go. I had not been in Stella's downstairs in many months, as we usually met in the garden or coming and going on the porch. I was confused. This was not the Stella's I knew.

Stella's house was a beautiful old Victorian that once belonged to Stella's family. The family was wealthy, but Stella was the black sheep and had been disinherited years ago. Somehow, she had managed to buy the house back. Fiercely independent, Stella had been an artist, a dancer and a suffragette, fighting for women's rights long before women were even able to vote.

The house had been restored to its original buttery yellow with green and purple trim. Twenty-foot high, ancient rhododendrons bordered the yard and the flowerbeds always had something blooming.

Stella and I had hit it off immediately. She wanted to rent her upstairs and I needed my own place. She needed help around the yard and I didn't have much money, but I could certainly do yard work. Her health was beginning to fail and I was a student nurse. It was a match made in heaven.

Stella's first floor had been filled with fascinating furniture, colorful wall hangings and many old photos. Above all, it was spotlessly clean and filled with light. What I saw now was a dark, cluttered hall, with mountains of newspapers and magazines stacked in odd ways, blocking the entrances to the other rooms.

Looking across the debris and into the kitchen, I could see the sink filled with dirty dishes and pots. The kitchen table was littered with soiled paper plates and remnants of half eaten meals. No wonder Stella couldn't find Eugene this morning. He could hide anywhere in this mess.

"Stella, what's happened to your house?" I asked. This was so unlike her.

"Oh Nora, I just can't keep up with everything anymore," she cried. "I didn't want you to see this. I planned to hire someone to help, but I just haven't gotten to it."

"Stella, I'm not sure if this is safe for you," I said. "Have you talked with Pamela lately?" Pamela was Stella's daughter with whom she didn't always get along.

"I don't want to talk with Pamela," she declared. "She's always telling me what to do. She's never any fun. She'll probably try to put me in one of those homes, like the one you work in."

"We need to talk with her, Stella," I said. "I'll talk with her for you."

"You do what you have to, Nora," said Stella, "but I'm not going to one of those homes."

I didn't want to argue. "I guess I'll go upstairs and pack a few things and make my calls up there," I said. "You go back inside and be careful."

My apartment had a separate entrance with an outside stairway. The railing was draped in climbing roses that bloomed all year long. The place had been renovated and furnished years before for one of Stella's many artist friends. I loved it. There was a small living room furnished with two plush red sofas and a curious collection of dark wood tables and cabinets. The walls in the apartment were white and adorned with colorful, modernistic paintings, which I guessed were the work of that previous tenant. I had added a few of my favorite seascapes—prints, of course—and a lot of family pictures.

The apartment had one bedroom with an old mahogany, canopied double bed, covered with numerous thick, colorful quilts and comforters. The kitchen had a tiny, two burner gas stove with an oven and there was a new refrigerator. A painted drop-leaf table with a built-in window bench had extra folding chairs for guests. What I liked best in the kitchen, however, was the breathtaking view of the harbor, when I can see it that is, as we often have fog.

As I walked into the apartment, I could see that the plumbers had removed the old water heater and left it sitting in the middle of my living room. They were in the process of putting in the new one. The carpet was soaked and it squished with each step I took. I walked across the room towards the kitchen, not sure if the flooring would hold or not. I picked up my address book and flipped to Pamela Ward's numbers, which I had for emergencies.

"Mrs. Ward? This is Nora Brady, your mother's upstairs tenant. We met several months ago."

"Hi, Nora," she said. "What can I do for you?" There was no warmth in Pamela Ward's voice. Maybe she expected me to complain about something.

"Mrs. Ward, I'm calling because I'm concerned about your mother." I outlined the day's events and told Mrs. Ward about the condition of her mother's house. I told her that I was unaware of this until today. I briefly wondered why Pamela wasn't aware of these conditions. Then I explained Stella's concern regarding being placed in a "home."

"I had no idea things had gotten so bad," said Mrs. Ward. "You know my mother. She doesn't let me do much. I try to let her call the shots."

"I know," I said.

"I'll try to get over in the next day or so," she said. "Thank you for calling." She had definitely warmed up. And I now understood that she was trying to let her mother be as independent as possible.

Next I placed a call to Tina, but she wasn't home yet. I left a message on her cell phone, asking if she could put me up for a few days. After that I packed a suitcase. I collected other items that I might need, like books and my dilapidated pillow which I can't live without. I didn't quite know what to do about the refrigerator. I took out what I thought might spoil and left the rest.

I went back downstairs to recheck Stella and to give her Tina's phone number. She apparently had gone back inside, as I'd encouraged her to do. I knocked on the door, but she didn't answer. I pushed open the front door, which Stella never locked and I called out her name. I wasn't sure, but I thought I heard a pounding coming from somewhere near the kitchen. I called her name again and started working my way towards the kitchen.

The pounding became louder and when I called out to Stella again, I heard a feeble response, followed by a low-pitched moaning. The moaning seemed to be coming from the far side of the kitchen, to the right. I thought that was where the bathroom was located, just before the back bedroom. I worked my way towards the bathroom door, again calling out to Stella. I heard the moaning much louder and definitely coming from the bathroom. The bathroom door was closed.

"Stella," I called. "Are you in the bathroom?"

"Yessss," came her response, followed by another pitiful moan.

"What happened, Stella?" I called through the bathroom door. "Can I come in to help you?"

"I can't get the door open," she said. "I fell and I'm up against the door."

"I'm going to go for some help, Stella," I called in. "Don't move."

I ran my eyes around the kitchen and found the phone on the opposite wall. I made my way across, with my feet sticking to the floor at every step. I called "911" and explained the situation. Then I ran back upstairs to see if the plumbers could help, but they had apparently finished for the day and were gone. I grabbed my own toolbox from under the kitchen sink and ran back downstairs.

I set my toolbox down outside the bathroom door and explained to Stella that help was on the way. Having noted that the bathroom door hinges were on the inside, I told Stella that I was going to try to come in through the bathroom window. I opened my toolbox, found a screwdriver and hammer and headed back out the front door, which I left open for the rescue team. I worked my way around the hedges in back and found the bathroom window.

Luckily it was open and luckily it was the old style window that was easy to push up. I hoisted myself onto the sill and nearly fell into the toilet on the other side. My eyes adjusted to the dim light in the bathroom and I saw Stella on the floor by the door. She was lying on her right side with her knees drawn up to her chin. She looked like a small child. So fragile.

"I'm here, Stella," I said, "and the firemen will be here any minute. Don't worry." I knelt down and touched her shoulder.

"Oh, Nora, I'm so stupid," said Stella.

"Just relax," I said.

There were only two hinges on the bathroom door. I slipped the screwdriver under the top knob of the first pin and angled the handle downwards. I then started tapping the handle of the screwdriver with the hammer and watched as the pin started to loosen. Several more taps and I had the first pin out of the door.

As I started working on the second pin, I could hear the fireman calling to us from the front porch. I shouted that we were in the bathroom and continued working on the second pin. When I heard the first of the firemen outside the door, I explained what had happened and what I was doing.

"Good start," he said. "We'll have someone in there in a minute to help you."

I kept talking to Stella to reassure her. A second fireman came in through the bathroom window and we had the door off in seconds. The emergency medical technicians arrived and began preparing a stretcher and setting up the cardiac monitor and oxygen in the kitchen. The firemen were talking calmly to Stella, but I couldn't hear her responses. They gently examined her and after deciding that she could be safely moved to the stretcher, they lifted her off the floor.

Stella screamed for an instant and then seemed to relax. As they settled her on the stretcher, I noticed there was a steady stream of blood coming from a cut above her right temple. One EMT was applying pressure and another was preparing a bandage. Now that Stella was on the stretcher, I could also see that she had fractured her right hip. Her right leg was definitely shorter than her left leg and her right toes were rotated outwards, classic signs of a hip fracture. Stella was not going to be happy.

As the emergency team prepared to take Stella out to the waiting ambulance, I attempted to reassure her. "Stella, don't worry," I said. "These guys will take really good care of you and I'll call Pamela."

"Don't forget Eugene," Stella said weakly. "Do you think I'll be gone very long?"

"I don't know, Stella," I said. "It looks like you might have broken your hip. If that's what it is, it's easy to fix, but any fracture takes a while to heal. Don't worry. I'll take very good care of Eugene."

I waited until Stella was safely in the ambulance and on her way to the hospital. I checked on Eugene's food and water. Then I called Pamela, who assured me that she would go to the hospital immediately. After that I called Tina again. This time she was home. "You'll never believe what just happened," I said. "Did you get my message?" I repeated my earlier story and then told her what had just happened to Stella.

"Wow, Nora, I hope that Stella's O.K.," said Tina. "I got your message and of course you can stay here for a few days since Mary's out of town. After that I'm not sure since our landlord is very strict about anyone else staying in the apartment. Don't worry though. We'll work something out."

I thanked Tina and said I would be at her apartment later that evening. Then I headed for the hospital to check on Stella.

Chapter 7

The next morning came too soon. I was tired and sore from sleeping on Tina's too short couch. I had stayed at the hospital until almost midnight, waiting to see Stella after her surgery. Pamela and her husband Charles were also waiting and that had helped to pass the time. Stella had fractured her pelvis as well as her hip. Her recovery was going to be a little slower than anticipated because there wasn't any good way to repair a fractured pelvis except with rest.

Pamela and I discussed what to do about Stella's house. Pamela promised to have a cleaning service come in while Stella was in the hospital. She also planned to arrange some regular part time help for Stella. It seemed likely that Stella would need to go to a nursing home after being in the hospital, at least for the early recovery period. She would need lots of therapy. Hopefully, Stella would come to Marian Manor where I could visit her more easily. At least she would have a familiar face and maybe she could even be placed on 2 West.

"Well, sleepyhead, now who's the late one," chirped Tina, as I walked into the nurses' station. We had come separately as we had different things to do after work. It was probably the first time Tina had ever arrived at work before me.

"I'm not late," I growled. "In fact, on my slowest days, I'm still faster than you!" We were waiting for morning report. Everyone was there and everyone seemed to be in a good mood, except for me.

"What happened to you?" asked Dominic.

I explained the situation with Stella and the joys of sleeping on Tina's couch.

"I have a spare room," said Deborah with an understanding smile. "You're welcome to use it for a few weeks, if you'd like."

I was too stunned to speak for a few moments and my mind was racing. I couldn't believe Deborah would actually make such an offer. At the same time, I couldn't believe how well this would fit into my plan to get to know her better.

"Deborah, that's so nice of you!" I exclaimed. "Are you sure? You hardly know me."

"I'm sure, Nora," said Deborah. "I know you're a nice person and that you take good care of things. My sisters are away at college, so I have the extra room."

I immediately felt guilty for all my negative thoughts about Deborah. "Well, I couldn't pay very much right now," I started to explain. "I'm not sure if I'll still have to pay my rent at Stella's."

"You don't have to pay me anything," said Deborah. "The room is sitting empty. Well as empty as a room is for kids away at college."

"Thank you," I said. "It would be really convenient staying with someone who works the same hours that I work. Where do you live?"

"On L Street, just the other side of Spring Street," she answered.

"Why you're only a few blocks from my place!" I exclaimed. "I didn't know we lived so close."

"We can talk more later," said Deborah. It was time for report.

I went through the morning feeling pretty lighthearted. The problems at Stella's house now seemed more of an adventure than a hassle. Even the fact that today was the day for the foot doctor. Each resident who is going to be seen must have a 15 minute foot soak beforehand, but the nurses' aides take care of that. It's just more paperwork for the nurses.

Lunchtime came and went and still Deborah and I hadn't had a chance to talk. I wasn't sure how soon I could impose on her, but considering my night on Tina's couch, the sooner the better. I was sitting at the nurses' station finishing up my charts, when Deborah pulled her med cart alongside the desk.

"Nora, I'm sorry we haven't had a chance to talk yet," she said. "Would you like to come by after work to see the room?"

"I'd love to," I said.

"You're welcome to stay tonight, if you want," said Deborah. "Actually, it would be nice if you were there this weekend, as I'm going away. You could take care of Pluto for me. Are you O.K. with dogs?"

I knew there was a catch. "I like dogs," I said, "but I'm kind of afraid of ones I don't really know."

"Pluto is a schnauzer," said Deborah. "They're noisy, but harmless. Pluto loves company and it would save me having to board him again. That gets pretty expensive, so you're actually saving me money."

"My friend Nancy used to raise schnauzers," I said. "They're usually pretty nice dogs, just very protective. I'll be fine with Pluto."

"I'm sure you will be," said Deborah.

"I'm going over to the hospital after work to check on Stella," I said. "Then I'll pick up my things at Tina's and check on Eugene. That's Stella's cat. Would it be alright if I come by after dinner, about 7:00?"

"You can come by any time," said Deborah. "I tend to go to bed early, though, so I hope it's before 9:00, if that's O.K."

"That's fine with me," I said. "Just let me get your phone number."

As I was reviewing and updating my charts at the end of the day, Jean leaned over the counter above me. "I just want to see if there were any new orders after the podiatrist was here this morning," she said, taking my clipboard. "And I wanted to say how sorry I was to hear about your friend's fall and your housing problem. I think it's very nice of you to accept Deborah's offer to help." She was scanning my notes, not looking at me.

"Nice of me?" I asked.

"Well you and Tina were talking about making more of an effort with Deborah," she said. "The best way to know someone is to live with them. My father always used to say, 'If you want to make a friend, let them do you a favor.'" She handed the clipboard back to me, smiled and walked off.

I thought about Jean's words as I ran my errands that evening. It didn't take me long at the hospital. Stella was very sleepy, but she wasn't in pain. We visited briefly and I tried to help her eat some dinner, but she kept dozing off. The nurse told me Stella had been out of bed with physical therapy and had done very well. They expected her to be ready to go home or to a rehabilitation facility within a week. Stella, of course, wanted to go home.

By the time I got to Deborah's, it was just after 7:00. I had stopped to pick up my things at Tina's and I had stopped to feed Eugene. Deborah's house was a small, inviting white bungalow with deep blue shutters and a beautiful garden. Deborah answered the door with a towel in her hands. She was just finishing the supper dishes and she offered me some dessert. We went through the living room and into the kitchen where I gratefully accepted the slice of raspberry pie, along with a cup of tea. The kitchen was small and cheery, with an old-fashioned red countertop, white frilly curtains and a small, worn, but highly polished round oak table. Pluto barked and jumped around when I first came in, but then he settled quietly at my feet.

"I should have asked if you'd had any supper," said Deborah. "I mean before I gave you that dessert."

"I stopped for a burger," I confessed. "I know it's not good for me, but I figure it's only for a short period of time, until I can cook my own food again." I can be very good with excuses.

"Well, let me show you around," said Deborah. "This is obviously the kitchen. Feel free to help yourself to anything in the frig. I only ask that you do your own dishes."

We then walked back into the small living room. There was, what appeared to be, a comfortable brown tweed couch with two worn, gold tweed armchairs. A country pine coffee table with matching end tables and brass table lamps completed the furnishings. In one corner were an old record player cabinet and a small color TV. Family pictures were displayed on one wall and there was a wonderful oil painting over the couch. It was a quiet redwood stand with light filtering through the upper branches of the trees to the forest floor.

"I love your painting," I said. "It's beautiful. Peaceful."

"Thank you," she said. "It's an Otto Schwarz. He was my grandfather. My mother's father. This was my parents' home. They were killed in an auto accident about ten years ago. We have quite a few of my grandfather's paintings, since my mother was an only child. This is my favorite."

We picked up my things by the front door and started down the hallway to the right. Deborah pointed out the bathroom, which was tiled in pink everywhere except the ceiling. "This is Rose and Jane's room," she said as she pointed to the next room on the left. "You can set your things in there. Then, this is my room and this is our craft or sewing room," she said as she indicated two more rooms on the right.

The sisters' room was a soft blue with lovely mahogany furniture and Deborah's room was lavender with a brass bed and rattan dresser. The craft room was cream colored and had two sewing machines and a big worktable. It looked like there were several projects in progress and that the room got a lot of use.

"I've made up Jane's bed for you," said Deborah. "That's the first one as you go into the room. I've also left towels in the bathroom. Yours are the green ones. If you need more, just help yourself."

"I can't tell you how much I appreciate this, Deborah," I said. "Just to be able to stretch out fully tonight will be wonderful. Where are you going this weekend, if you don't mind my asking?"

"It's parents' weekend at UC and I usually try to be there for my sisters," she answered. "I'll probably drive down after work on Friday, so I have all day Saturday to visit with them."

"Sounds like you're a good sister," I said. "I could take some lessons. What do you do to relax?"

"As you can see, I do a lot of sewing, for myself and for other people too," she replied, "like the Jacobsport Repertory Theater. I also paint, but I'm not very good."

By this time I was having terrible pangs of guilt. How could I have thought Deborah capable of stealing or harming anyone? Here was a woman who obviously cared for her family, worked hard and did not appear to have any financial needs. She was also generous. After all she had opened her door to a near total stranger. Me.

"Well, goodnight Nora. See you in the morning," said Deborah. "By the way, there's an alarm clock on the bedside table. You're welcome to stay up and watch TV, or whatever, but I'm tired."

"Thanks again, Deborah," I said. "I don't know how I can thank you enough."

"Don't worry about it," said Deborah. "I know you'd do the same for me. Now sleep well." She then went back to turn off the lights in the kitchen, but left a low light on in the living room. I closed the door to the sisters' bedroom, pulled my suitcase onto Rose's bed, got out my nightshirt and hung up my clothes for work. I was ready for a good night's sleep, but it was too early for me. I changed my clothes and went back to the living room to watch TV.

When I finally did go to bed, sleep would not come. First, I got to thinking about my own family. Hearing about Deborah's family made me a bit homesick for my own. I'm right in the middle of two boys and two girls, but they're all back in the Berkshires of Massachusetts. We only get together a few times a year, but we do talk on the phone and send e-mails. I love my family, but I love my independence too.

My dad was in the lumber business. We moved to Jacobsport when he got a good offer from one of the mills. When the lumber business in the northwest started to dry up, he moved the family back to the Berkshires. Now he runs a hardware store. My mom works part-time in a nursing home. I miss them, but I love living here by the water.

I also kept thinking about the recent thefts and the questions surrounding the death of Melba Jones. At first, I had been sure that Lonnie was the thief, but then Jean's defense of Lonnie made me abandon that possibility. Then, I was sure that Deborah must be involved, since she always seemed to be ill just after a theft occurred. I didn't know how that connected exactly, but it seemed suspicious. Now, I just couldn't imagine Deborah stealing. So who could it be?

It had to be someone with easy access to the residents. That meant it would have to be a nurse, a nurses' aide, or a cleaning person. It couldn't be anyone from the kitchen, because they almost never went into a resident's room. I ran down the list of people who worked on 2 West and carefully considered each person. No one seemed likely.

What about one of the administrative people? Could it be another resident or family member, as Detective Maguire had suggested? My mind was spinning. I would have to think about these others tomorrow. Finally, I drifted off into a troubled sleep. I dreamt of chasing phantom figures, down never-ending hallways, never actually seeing anyone's face. A mist swirled around the disappearing figures and Detective Maguire's head kept bobbing in and out of this mist.

Chapter 8

The next morning I found Deborah already up and dressed when I rolled out of bed and made my way to the kitchen. She was having coffee and offered me a cup. I helped myself and joined her at the kitchen table. As I glanced at the clock, I saw it was only 6:00 a.m., plenty of time to get ready for work. Pluto barely lifted his head from his position at Deborah's feet. It looked like he and I were going to get along fine.

"How did you sleep?" asked Deborah.

"Like a log," I lied. "I think all these problems of the last few days have caught up with me." This was not a lie.

"What do you mean?" asked Deborah.

"Well, aside from the problems with Stella and not having an apartment at the moment," I explained, "these thefts and the death of Melba Jones have really bothered me."

"It's bothered me too," said Deborah. "Any ideas?"

"I don't know," I answered. "I keep mulling over the possibilities, but I get no answers." I could hardly tell Deborah she had been at the top of my list of suspects.

"I can't imagine who would do such things," said Deborah.

"I guess Detective Maguire's got his job cut out for him," I said. "And I had better get ready for mine, if I want to keep it." I got up from the table and rinsed my cup in the sink. As I showered and dressed for work, I continued to replay the week's events. I wondered if Deborah had considered me a suspect? Why not?

"Nora," called Deborah. "I forgot to give you a key. I'll leave one on the kitchen table. I'm going on to work. Just lock up when you leave."

"Thanks again, Deborah," I called. "I'll be along shortly."

Finishing my morning beauty ritual with a quick brush through my hair and a dash of lipstick, I formulated my plan for the day. I decided to take a look at work schedules. I wanted to see who was on duty around the time of the thefts. I guessed Detective Maguire was looking at the same things, but maybe I would see something he didn't. It was worth a shot.

The nurses' station was in turmoil when I arrived. Several of the night staff were in tears and Jean was talking intently with Ruth Rice. Tina and Deborah were sitting down with their clipboards. They glanced at me, but didn't speak. Dominic, Tara and Lonnie were nowhere to be seen.

"What's happening," I asked.

"June Michaels passed away last night," said Tina. "The night staff is very upset. The aides went to console some of the residents who are just getting the news."

I sank into the nearest chair, resting my head in my hands. I felt like a 20-foot breaker had hit me. I wasn't close to Mrs. Michaels, but I had liked her. It was difficult to believe she was dead. And she hadn't been ill. That she should die so shortly after the theft of her jewelry, just like Melba Jones, was too much coincidence. For the first time, I felt afraid. Not for myself, but for our residents. Undoubtedly, we had another coroner's case and there would be more questions from the police.

I looked up at the sound of many footsteps coming down the hall. There was Sam and Iris Clayton, Anne Dixon, Jimmy Ramirez and Detective Maguire, all together.

"Let's use the conference room," said Jean, motioning the others down the hall.

I looked at the others. "Maybe we should just go ahead and get started on our regular assignments," I said, but my heart wasn't in it.

"That sounds like a good idea to me," said Deborah. "I'll find the aides and let them know. We need to keep things moving along for the other residents." At that, she got up and headed towards her section.

"Well you two are certainly chummy," said Tina, not unkindly.

"I think I was wrong about Deborah," I said. "She really has her hands full, taking care of her sisters. And it's kind of her to put me up."

"Well, I hope it answers some of your questions," said Tina, getting up. "I'm going to get started with my team."

I sat alone at the desk for a few minutes. I still couldn't believe Mrs. Michaels had died. I knew there were a few residents on my team that were close to her and they would be very upset. I was particularly concerned about Mrs. Danner. I would check on her first. Then I wanted to take a look at those staff schedules.

Mrs. Danner was up and dressed and sitting alone in a chair by the window in her room. She didn't even look up when I entered. I walked over to her and placed my hand on her shoulder. "Mrs. Danner, I'm so sorry for your loss," I said. "I know you and Mrs. Michaels were close."

"I just can't believe she's gone. Oh, I know that at my age I should expect my friends to be dying, but this was so sudden," she said. "You know she was worried that something else would happen after her letter opener was stolen."

"No, I didn't know she was worried," I said. "I just thought she was still upset about the theft. You do know that it wasn't only the letter opener, don't you?"

"Yes, I know about the necklace," she said, looking up at me with tears welling in her eyes. "June told me. She was so concerned that something like this might happen to me."

I sat down on the bed next to her chair and neither of us said anything for a few minutes. We looked out the window where men were trimming trees on the back lawn.

"You know the police are working very hard to find the thief," I explained. "And you also know that Mrs. Michaels' heart wasn't doing too well. Maybe, the stress was too much."

"I know all this, but it doesn't help," she said. "I just miss her already. We talked about everything. You know it's hard to find somebody to talk with that really understands what you mean, especially when you get to be our age."

"I guess it would be," I said. I didn't know what else to say and I didn't want to get up, in case Mrs. Danner wanted to talk some more. The most I could do was listen. Sometimes that's the only thing a nurse can do.

"Don't worry about me," said Mrs. Danner. "I just need some time to myself. I'll come down to the dining room later."

"Why don't I bring you some tea and toast?" I asked.

"That would be lovely, dear," she said. "Thank you for checking on me."

I walked back into the hall and nearly ran into Tina, who was coming to find me. "Sam is calling a nursing staff meeting, now, in the conference room," she said. "The aides will finish serving breakfast and Jean will meet with them later."

"I'll be there in just a minute," I said. "Let me get this tea and toast for Mrs. Danner."

The conference room was nearly full when I walked in. There were staff nurses from all the units, as well as the therapists, nurse managers and Mrs. Dixon. The room was about the size of two resident rooms with white walls and a bank of windows along one side. There were three computer terminals at the back of the room and a large screen and projector at the front. The folding metal tables had been moved and folding metal chairs had been set up for the staff. There was one table up front where the Claytons were sitting with Jimmy Ramirez. Detective Maguire joined them and he was introducing a pretty blond woman I didn't recognize.

A grim faced Sam Clayton called us to order and then introduced the others at the table. Apparently the new woman was also a police officer. Her name was Caitlyn Cruise. "I'm sure you're all aware of the serious problems we're facing this morning. We've had two major thefts, followed by the deaths of these same two residents, all within a couple of days. While the thefts are serious, the deaths do appear to be from natural causes. Just coincidental. We're awaiting the autopsy reports. He nodded towards Jimmy.

"Now we're starting to get calls from the newspapers," Sam continued, "and we're getting calls from families who wish to move our residents to other facilities. If you have any information whatsoever that you can share with the police, we need you to do this. The smallest bit of information could be invaluable."

Sam Clayton sat down and Detective Maguire stood up. "In the interest of preventing further thefts, we are instituting some new measures," he said. "First, we're asking that anything you bring to work be in a clear plastic bag. If that's a problem, please talk with your nurse manager, or with any of us. Second, we're telling you that you may be asked to empty your pockets at any time. This is not just for nurses. It will be for the entire staff until such time as the thief is apprehended. Any questions?"

No one raised a hand. Detective Maguire sat down and Mrs. Dixon, the Director of Nursing, stood up. Anne Dixon was a big lady with perfect posture from her years in the Air Force. She had a cheerful face with strong cheekbones reflecting her Native American ancestry. Her dark hair, beginning to gray, was perfectly styled.

"I know this is a difficult time for everyone, especially the nursing staff on 2 West," she began. "We must pull together. We've always provided excellent care to our residents and we must continue to do so despite whatever we hear in the community. The managers will explain these new measures to the remaining staff later today. I hope each of you will do your part. Please feel free to come and talk with me at any time, if you have any questions or concerns." She looked around the room and then sat down.

"If no one has any questions, you're free to go," said Sam Clayton. "We know you have a lot to do and we appreciate your help. As Mrs. Dixon said, please feel free to come to any of us with questions or concerns. Thanks for your time and efforts."

No one moved for several moments. It was as if the words from the meeting had weighted us down like fresh cement. When the group did begin to move, no one talked. The only sounds were the rustle of clothes and an occasional chair scraping the floor.

As we looked around at each other, we just as quickly looked away. Suspicion saturated the air like a June fog. One of us was a thief. But who?

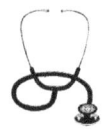

Chapter 9

I finished the day with a heavy heart and was collecting my things to go home, when Mrs. Dixon came onto the unit. "Oh, Nora, just who I was looking for," she said. "Do you have a minute?"

"Of course," I said. "I was just getting ready to leave."

"I received a call today from a Pamela Ward," she said.

"Yes, my landlady's daughter," I said.

"Well, her mother is going to require placement in a nursing home," said Mrs. Dixon, "until she's fully recovered and able to be home on her own. They would like to have Mrs. Margoles on your unit and I wanted to talk with you first. Sometimes it's awkward to have someone we know under our care."

"That's fine with me," I said. "I'd love having Stella up here. The only open room is on the other end. That's even better. I can be more of a friend."

"Wonderful," said Mrs. Dixon. "I'll call Mrs. Ward and tell her we'll hold a bed for Mrs. Margoles. Thanks for your input, Nora. By the way, how's your rotation going? You students are such a help to us and I've heard good things about both you and Tina."

"It's going well, Mrs. Dixon," I replied. "Thanks for asking. I'm just on my way over to see Stella now. I can share the good news with her, although I know she's not going to be happy. She hates the thought of a nursing home. But, maybe since she knows I'm here, it will be easier for her."

"I hope so," said Mrs. Dixon. "Good luck." She started down the hall towards 2 East.

As I gathered up my things to leave, I suddenly remembered the work schedules I wanted to go over. They were kept in a green binder by the telephone. Fortunately, the binder was sitting right where it was supposed to be. I pulled the current and the last schedules out of the binder and quickly made copies. I slipped these into an empty folder sitting on the desk. I would look at the schedules later, when I had more time to study them.

I arrived at the hospital just as the physical therapist was getting Stella up to walk in the hall for the second time that day. "I'll walk along with you," I said. "I'm looking forward to seeing how well you're doing."

"I'm not doing well at all," said Stella. "I can't do anything for myself."

"Now that's not true, Stella," said the physical therapist. "You've been getting up with very little assistance and we hardly helped with your shower today. You're doing very well for two days post-op."

"What do you know?" asked Stella. "I'm used to cleaning my house, mowing my lawn and caring for my Eugene. I can't do any of that now," said Stella, as she slowly rolled her walker down the hall. Her walk was steady and she didn't seem to be in pain.

After the walk, I stayed to visit with Stella. I reassured her again that I was checking on Eugene every day. I also told her the news about her coming to Marian Manor. As predicted, she wasn't happy.

"Nursing homes are places where people go to die," she said. "I'm not ready to die."

"People also come to recover after surgery," I explained. "We have people of all ages at Marian Manor, with all kinds of problems. The staff is really nice. I think you'll like it there and it's only for a few weeks."

"Will you be my nurse?" asked Stella.

"Well, I'll be on the same unit," I said, "but it's usually better if the nurse is someone you don't know very well. She can see things that a friend or relative might not see. Besides, you know, I'm still only a student."

"What kind of things do they see?" asked Stella. "No one is going to see anything I don't want them to see."

"Things like whether you're eating like you should be, or doing as much for yourself as you should be," I explained. "Sometimes families or friends are too easy on a patient. They don't want to hurt or upset the patient."

"Well, if I have to do this, I'm glad, at least, that you'll be there," said Stella.

"Me too," I said.

"Now, I can still go home after I'm better, right?" asked Stella.

"Of course," I replied.

"And you're not moving, are you?" asked Stella. "I mean your apartment will be fixed up and I want you to stay there."

"Why would you ask that?" I exclaimed. "I love my apartment and I love having you for my landlady. Hopefully you'll be home in a few weeks, but you will still need some help, you know."

"What kind of help?" asked Stella.

"You'll probably need a home health nurse and a therapist for a little while, and an aide to help with your bath," I explained. "You're also going to need someone to help with your housework. You know you haven't been able to keep up with that."

"I know," said Stella. "But the thought of all these strange people coming into my house. I don't like that idea at all."

"They're professionals," I said. "They're only there to make your life easier. They don't come for very long, just long enough to do the job that needs to be done."

"We'll see," said Stella.

We said our good-bys and I headed over to Stella's house to check on Eugene. As I approached the house I saw a white van sitting in the driveway with several men walking back and forth from the house, carrying large bundles. As I drew nearer, I could see a sign on the side of the van that said "Northcoast Cleaning Company."

I parked on the street and walked up the short sidewalk. One man was coming out, carrying a bundle of what looked like old newspapers. I introduced myself and explained my reason for being there.

"I saw that cat when we first went in," he said, "but I haven't seen it all day. We're just finishing up, but we'll have to come back tomorrow. Today we just collected rubbish. Tomorrow we'll clean."

When I walked through the front door, I couldn't believe the difference from two days ago. "You have to hand it to Pamela," I thought. "When she says she's going to do something, she does it." While the place still needed serious cleaning, I could once again see the beautiful furniture and rugs, and there was no trouble walking through to the kitchen. I could also see that repair work had started on the ceiling.

I called to Eugene, but he didn't appear. Then I rattled the food packets, but still there was no "swoosh" of fur gliding around the corner. I searched and finally found him hiding under Stella's bed. I carefully coaxed him out with a few treats, as I sat on the rocking chair beside the bed. Then, to my surprise, he jumped into my lap and started purring. While I knew very little about cats, I took this to be a good sign.

I rocked Eugene for a while until both of us were nearly asleep. Then I roused myself and went to fill his dishes. Next, I headed upstairs to pick up a few more things from my own apartment. When I left, Eugene seemed satisfied and was eating eagerly from the dish I had filled.

Upstairs, my apartment seemed somewhat better than when I had left. The new hot water heater was in place and when I checked the faucet, the water was nice and hot. The rug had been pulled up from the floor and there was a dehumidifier running on the floor to help dry it out. While the floor did look drier, it was obviously going to be a few more days before I could return. Fortunately, the floor didn't need to be replaced. I decided to call Pamela to see if she knew when the apartment would be ready.

"Pamela? Hi, this is Nora," I said. "How are you?"

"Oh, Nora," she replied. "More importantly, how are you after that long night?"

"I'm fine, thanks," I said. "I'm here at the house and I just wanted to check to see if you knew when I could move back into my apartment?"

"No, I don't know," said Pamela, "but I'll find out and get back to you." I gave her my work number and Deborah's number.

My last task before going back to Deborah's was to pick up my mail. Pamela picked up Stella's mail. Among the usual junk and bills, I spotted some familiar handwriting and I smiled. It was something from my Mom and I always enjoyed mail from home. Even though we talk on the phone all the time, or send e-mails, it's still nice to get snail mail. My Mom and Dad were planning a trip west and were hoping to spend some time with me. They knew a lot of people in Jacobsport, so I never had to worry about entertaining them. I decided to call home.

Later, when I got to Deborah's, I found that she had gone out for the evening. She left a note saying that she had some shopping to do for her trip to UC and then she was going to see a movie. I decided to go back out, pick up some Chinese carryout and then study the work schedules while I had the evening to myself.

I poured over the schedules as I picked at my Kung Pao chicken. I hadn't been as hungry as I thought. Try as I might, I could not see any relationship between the events at Marian Manor and the staffing, even when I considered all the shifts. I made myself a chart depicting the dates of the thefts, or at least when the thefts were noted and the dates of the deaths that had occurred. I blocked out whoever was off on the days surrounding those dates.

Deborah was off both days the thefts were discovered. Dominic was off the day Mrs. Michaels' theft was discovered. Both Deborah and Dominic were working the days that Melba Jones and June Michaels died, but only Dominic was working both days before the two deaths. There didn't seem to be any pattern whatsoever for the other staff or the other shifts. Also, we didn't really know when the first theft occurred; Mrs. Jones couldn't tell us. Furthermore, we didn't know if the theft of Mrs. Jones' jewelry was the first theft. I was getting a headache.

As I sat back in my chair to study the chart again, I heard Deborah's key in the front door. I quickly slid the schedules and chart back into the folder and opened a magazine that was sitting on the table. I went back to picking at my dinner. I felt guilty, but I wasn't ready to share my thoughts on all this just yet.

"You're home early," I said, as Deborah came in. "You must not have gone to the movie."

"No, I did my shopping, grabbed a bite to eat, but then decided I was too tired to sit through a movie," said Deborah. "How was your evening?"

I told her about my talk with Mrs. Dixon and my visit to Stella. After this past week, who knew what surprises we would find tomorrow? When we said goodnight, I just hoped I could sleep. I didn't want another night of chasing phantoms.

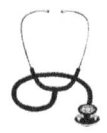

Chapter 10

Friday morning. I was so happy to be off on the weekend. I was discouraged and I wanted a break. I was disappointed that the schedules hadn't given me any clues. I was missing my apartment and Pamela Ward had not called to tell me how soon I could go back. It seemed that everyone at work was irritable.

Tina would be training this weekend for the marathon, which was scheduled for next weekend. Deborah was going to see her sisters at UC. Mary and Erin, my other two friends, were planning to attend a respiratory disease workshop. I wasn't sure what I was going to do with myself. Maybe I would call Jimmy Ramirez and see if he still was interested in playing some golf.

In the meantime, I still had today. Things were quiet at the moment, but what every nurse quickly learns, is that you never say the "Q" word. You never say that it's quiet. As sure as you say it, or sometimes even if you think it, everything will go crazy. This was simply a lull. A few days when none of the residents are very sick, when no one is complaining very much and when all the charting is up to date.

I completed the morning meds and treatments and decided to take a walk down the hall to see how everyone was doing. I thought I could help the aides with the morning baths, but even the aides were caught up. Nurses always say they don't have enough time to talk with patients and it's often true. Sometimes we have the time, however, and we either don't have the energy, or we've forgotten how to just sit down and visit with a patient. Maybe we also worry about whether someone else will think of something for us to do, if we don't look busy enough.

I started at the far end of the hall. The first room was empty. The ladies in the next three rooms were busy sorting through their closets. I stopped at each room and asked how everyone was doing. They all seemed to be deep in conversation regarding laundry products, grandchildren and ailments. Mr. Lowenstein wasn't in his room. He was probably downstairs with Mr. Jessel and Mr. Parker. These three had become inseparable. Clark Skinner was dozing in his chair by the window and Charlotte Danner was on the telephone. There was no one to talk with me.

When I went back to the nurses' station, the other nurses were working on their charts and denied the need for my help. The aides were taking residents down to activities, finishing up on baths, or they were on break. I decided maybe now was a good time to catch up on some reading in the library. I checked with Tina to see if she would monitor my team while I was gone and this was fine with her.

The library was really just one end of another conference room located next to the Clayton's office on the first floor. It was nothing like the conference room on 2 West. The table and chairs were a polished walnut with floral seat covers that matched the drapes. The carpeting was a thick gray green that muffled most sounds in the room and the pale green walls reflected the light, making the room a pleasant place to work. There was a wall of books and journals at one end of the room, along with two comfortable, raspberry colored armchairs and two brass reading lamps. I picked up the most recent copies of two journals that I didn't receive at home. Then I sank into one of the armchairs.

I was just getting into the second journal when I heard a door slam in Sam's office next door. Then I heard two voices arguing. It was obvious they were trying to keep the volume down, but they were angry. It sounded like Sam and Iris. They didn't notice that when they slammed the main door to their office, the connecting door to the library popped open a crack. I didn't want to interrupt and embarrass them, since they were obviously in the middle of an argument.

"I'm not touching the Allen account!" said the man's voice.

"You have to do it, Sam, or there won't be any money available in the checking account for next week's payroll," said the woman's voice.

"We're already in way over our heads, Iris," said Sam. "If you keep pushing this, we will both end up in jail and lose Marian Manor. Is that what you want to happen?"

"I think you're being too dramatic, Sam," said Iris. "We're just moving money around. It's no different from what we've always done in the past."

"But we've always studied our investments carefully," said Sam. "This is gambling with our whole future."

"Don't be such a wimp, Sam," said Iris. "This is a good investment." There was a long pause in the conversation. I imagined they were staring at each other, waiting for the other to speak. When Sam said nothing, Iris continued in a softer voice. "Sam, I appreciate your concerns, but I don't think we have a choice. I'm going over to the bank now. I think I left the papers in the conference room."

"Now what?" I thought to myself. I pulled my feet up into the chair and tried to curl up. Maybe Iris wouldn't see me. Then the journal fell from my lap just as Iris came through the door from Sam's office. She was sure to have heard it. I was trapped! I rolled off the chair as I bent down to pick up the journal. I rose to see Iris standing at the other end of the conference table. Our eyes met and I felt a sudden chill run through me. I couldn't think of anything to say.

Iris was tall and thin and dark. Her straight black hair was hanging loose on her shoulders. Her clothes screamed expensive and the diamond earrings and multiple bracelets she wore were an echo. Iris looked down at the conference room table and started running her finger along the edge. "Well, this is very awkward," she said.

"What?" said Sam, coming into the room. "Nora?" he said, seeing me at the other end. Iris glared at him. "Oh," he said, suddenly understanding.

"Nora appears to have been eavesdropping on our conversation," said Iris.

"No!" I exclaimed. "I just didn't know how to tell you I was here. Everything happened too fast."

"Well, I hope you will keep this to yourself, Nora," said Sam. "It was a private conversation."

"Of course," I replied.

Iris was studying me. She turned to Sam. "I must have left those papers in my car," she said. Without saying anything further, she walked back into the office. Sam gave me a weak smile and followed her. He closed the door behind them. Tightly.

After they left, I sat down. Drained. What did their argument mean? Was Marian Manor having money problems? Was "the Allen account" connected with Harriet Allen? Were Sam and Iris involved in something illegal? Did this have anything to do with the thefts?

I got up and returned the journals to their proper shelves. I wished there was someone I could talk with about this, but I couldn't think of anyone. Besides, I had told Sam I would keep the conversation private.

I went back upstairs to 2 West, where the residents were getting ready for lunch. Tina was setting up her noon meds. "Learn anything new?" she asked.

"I looked over a couple of journals I don't get at home," I replied. "It's hard to keep up with everything in nursing."

"I don't keep up with the journals like you do," said Tina. "I think they're so expensive."

"Well, some are expensive," I said, "but not all of them and not any more than paying for a few workshops. This way I can study at home, at my leisure."

"Still, I admire you for keeping up," said Tina. "I should subscribe to at least one. Which do you recommend?"

We discussed the pros and cons of the nursing journals. Jean passed through and added her comments. Then she asked, "Would either of you have some extra time this afternoon to help Dr. Graves with her rounds? She only has about five residents to see."

"I should have the time," I said. "I'd be happy to round with her. What time will she be here?"

"It should be shortly after lunch," said Jean. "I have another meeting, so I really appreciate your helping out with this."

"No problem," I said.

"By the way, Nora," added Jean. "I forgot to tell you that Stella Margoles will be moving in this weekend, if all goes well. The hospital just called."

"That's great," I said. "It looked like she was doing very well when I saw her last night."

"We'll put her in June Michaels' old room," said Jean. "I hope that's O.K. with you."

"That's fine," I said.

Jean took off for her meeting and I decided to go to lunch so I'd be ready for the rounds with Dr. Graves. This was O.K. with Tina since everything was still "quiet." When I got back from lunch, I started to pull the charts for rounds.

Dr. Graves arrived on schedule. She was one of the newer doctors and no one had quite decided what they thought of her. She was young and pretty and she always wore long skirts, sandals and a different earring in each ear. She also had a diamond stud on one side of her nose. We knew she had a new baby at home. She seemed to know what she was doing, but she didn't explain anything. We always had to ask why we were doing the things she ordered.

We had just finished seeing the third resident. Dr. Graves was standing in the hall making a note in the chart when suddenly she threw her pen. It splintered as it hit the edge of the nurses' station. "I am not going to fill out any more of these forms," she said. "This is the biggest waste of my time."

"But, Dr. Graves," I said. "They have to be done by the resident's doctor."

"I don't care," said Dr. Graves. "I didn't go to school for the last eight years to waste my time on this." She started towards the fourth resident's room.

"Well, maybe you'd like to talk with Mrs. Dixon," I said. "She's always willing to take suggestions."

"Are you trying to tell me what to do?" asked Dr. Graves. "A student nurse?"

"No, Dr. Graves," I replied. "But we do try to work as a team."

"Is that sarcasm?" asked Dr. Graves. "I am a team player. Where I come from, everyone charts on the same notes and they're able to do this at Harrison Hospital. What's wrong with you people?" Harrison Hospital was our local hospital.

We were seeing Mr. Skinner at that moment and I didn't wish to argue with Dr. Graves in front of a resident. I was not happy, however, to be accused of sarcasm when I was only trying to be helpful. "Perhaps we can discuss this further when we finish rounds," I said to Dr. Graves.

"We certainly will discuss this further," said Dr. Graves. "I plan to discuss this with Jean and with Mrs. Dixon. You're not very helpful and I don't like your attitude. Why don't I have a real nurse doing rounds with me?"

At that, I walked out of Mr. Skinner's room and straight over to Jean's office. Jean had just returned from her meeting. "Perhaps you had better finish rounds with Dr. Graves," I said.

Jean gave me a puzzled look, but she didn't say anything. She got up and walked over to Mr. Skinner's room and joined Dr. Graves. They finished the rounds while I went on to pass my afternoon meds.

"Nora, we're ready to talk if you have a minute," said Jean, a little while later.

"I really don't have time for this," said Dr. Graves, "but I also don't have time for student nurses who get snippy with me."

"What exactly is the problem?" asked Jean.

"Dr. Graves had some comments regarding the forms," I began.

"Dr. Graves is able to speak for herself," said Dr. Graves. "I said I wasn't going to fill out all these forms and this student here tries to tell me how I should do my job."

"I suggested that Dr. Graves talk with Mrs. Dixon," I said to Jean.

"You said I wasn't a team player," said Dr. Graves. "I don't have time for sarcasm."

"In all fairness, Dr. Graves" said Jean, "Nora volunteered to do rounds with you and I'm sure she didn't intend to be sarcastic. Maybe you could give me your suggestions and I'll take them to the next managers' meeting."

Dr. Graves didn't respond. She seemed to be struggling with what she wanted to say next. "Alright, Jean. It's been a hectic day at the end of a hectic week. Perhaps I was too critical." She didn't say anything to me.

"Everyone is a bit irritable this week," said Jean. This was giving Dr. Graves more sympathy than I was willing to give at that moment. There are some doctors who feel that it's O.K. to fly off the handle at a nurse anytime they want to. I believe in second chances, but I also believe in apologies and I didn't hear one right now. Nurses have hectic days too.

It was people like Dr. Graves who made me question my decision to become a nurse—people who treat us like servants. Once I mentioned this to a college advisor who told me: "Nursing is like anything else, Nora. You make it what you want it to be." I learned that to be respected, you must demand respect and that has put me in hot water more than once in my short career. Even though nurses are the biggest part of the health care team, not everyone on the team recognizes their importance. When you stand up for yourself or your beliefs, you may be considered disobedient or a troublemaker. On the other hand, most of the residents that I see everyday, remind me of all the good reasons for being a nurse.

Jean said nothing more about the incident with Dr. Graves and I said nothing further about it to the other nurses. I stopped at the hospital on my way home and visited with Stella for an hour or so. Then I dragged myself back to Deborah's. Thank goodness it was Friday. But what was I going to do this weekend?

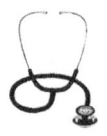

Chapter 11

"Hey Nora," shouted a friendly voice. I looked around the parking lot at the municipal golf course. Then I looked down the hill and spotted Jimmy Ramirez standing with two other guys on the first tee. I had taken the plunge and called Jimmy last night to see if he was still interested in playing some golf. He had already set up a 7:00 tee time for Saturday morning and, as it turned out, he was looking for a fourth player.

I waved hello and motioned that I was going up to the clubhouse to sign in. When I walked down the hill to join them, the "others" turned out to be Dan Maguire and Jason Montgomery, another friend of Jimmy's that I knew. Jason worked in a local sporting goods store. He was a friendly, redheaded guy known locally as a star athlete.

"Now, I have to warn you guys that I haven't played in quite a while," I said.

"Me either," said Dan Maguire.

I knew from the first that this was probably not my best decision. These guys were definitely good and I was definitely rusty. My long shots were straight, but short. I knew I was slowing the guys down, but they didn't seem to mind. I did do fairly well when it came to putting and I enjoyed playing. I was going to feel it the next day, though, as my arm muscles told me I wasn't in shape. The weather, however, was fantastic—warm and sunny with only a faint breeze, carrying the scent of nearby flowers. It was worth everything just to be outside.

By the time we finished the first nine holes, the course was getting pretty crowded. We stopped at the clubhouse for a late breakfast before playing the back nine. The guys ordered the full breakfast, but I just had a muffin and orange juice. We took a table that looked out over the back nine. Dan and I sat across from Jimmy and Jason.

"So how are things going over at Marian Manor?" asked Jimmy. "This has been quite a week for all of you, hasn't it?"

"Oh, yeh, I heard about that," said Jason. "What's going on?"

"It's been difficult," I said. "I don't think anyone really knows what's going on. I'm not sure if I'm supposed to talk about this," I said turning to Detective Maguire. I hadn't quite gotten used to calling him "Dan."

"Sure you can talk, Nora," he answered, "within limits. If you knew something critical to the investigation, you would have told the police. The police would then have told you not to mention whatever it was that you knew. You don't know anything, do you?" he asked with a slight smile.

"The problem with something like this is," I started to explain, wondering briefly if Dan was able to read minds, "is that everyone starts looking suspicious. Every little thing seems to hold a double meaning. We're all pretty irritable."

"Hey Nora," said Jason, who was looking over the morning paper. "You should be interested in this." He was holding up the front page of the *Jacobsport Times*, the local newspaper. The headline read: "Thefts and Deaths at Local Nursing Home." Dan and I reached across the table for the newspaper at the same time.

"I'll share it with you," said Dan.

The article would have scared a hardened criminal. It detailed the thefts. Then it raised questions not only about the recent deaths at Marian Manor, but also about deaths in the past. The paper demanded a state investigation. It hinted that Marian Manor had serious financial problems. It even said there were rumors about labor unions, that the staff was most unhappy. This was simply not true. While some facts may have been accurate, they were twisted.

"I've got to go over there," I said, starting to get up. "Everyone is going to be really upset. Where do newspapers get this stuff?"

"Stuff like this sells," said Dan, getting up. "I'm going over there with you. We can take my truck and I'll bring you back for your car later."

"But why are you going?" I asked.

"Well, shouldn't the issue of financial problems interest the police?" asked Dan.

Jimmy and Jason decided to continue onto the back nine, even if it meant taking on two new players. "Don't work too hard," said Jimmy.

"Say hi to my sister," said Jason.

"Your sister?" I asked, surprised.

"Lisa," said Jason.

"I didn't know you two were related," I said. "O.K." I should have guessed they were related now that I stopped to think about it—the same red hair and big smiles. Nice family. "Just let me change these shoes," I said to Dan as we walked to the parking lot.

"I'll change mine and pick you up at your car," said Dan as he headed towards his truck. Within minutes we were on the road to Marian Manor.

"Whoever wrote this had some inside information," I said. "Why would someone do something like this? Doesn't the paper know what this can do to the residents? What about all the good staff? All the good things we do?"

"The press really only cares about a good story and this is a good story," said Dan. "Everyday good deeds don't make headlines. Mystery makes headlines. Besides, the press doesn't need much to go on. Someone on staff probably made some innocent comment to a friend and the story ballooned from there."

I knew what Dan was saying made sense, but I didn't like it. When we arrived at Marian Manor the visitors' parking lot was full. This was unusual for a Saturday morning. When Dan and I walked in, it was obvious from some of the expressions that I saw that some people were surprised to see us together.

"I'm going up to 2 West," I said to Dan.

"And I'm going to try and talk with Sam and Iris Clayton," said Dan eyeing the line of people waiting outside Sam's office door.

Good luck," I said as I walked away.

"I don't need luck," said Dan to no one in particular. "I've got this." He pulled out his badge and flashed it to the first few people at the back of the line. The crowd parted for him.

Upstairs, everything seemed quiet. There was no one at the nurses' station. Staffing was always a bit lighter on weekends because there were few doctors visiting and no therapies. It could still be busy, though, as families often take residents out on the weekends. Getting residents ready for this could be quite time consuming.

I wandered down the hall and found some of the aides helping patients get dressed, but I still didn't see a nurse. I walked back up towards the dining room and saw that Lisa Duncan was in passing meds. When she saw me, her face lit up. She was always so friendly.

"We just can't keep you out of here, can we?" said Lisa. It was more statement than question.

"I wanted to see how everyone was doing," I said. "Oh, by the way, Jason said to say hi!"

"Jason?" asked Lisa. "Where did you see him?"

"We were playing golf this morning," I explained, "and then he saw this article in the paper. I had to see what was happening."

"What's happening?" asked Lisa.

"I'll wait until you finish passing meds," I said. It's not a good thing to interrupt a nurse while she's passing meds. It's easy to make mistakes if you're distracted.

I stepped out to the nurses' station to wait. Several other staff and a few residents came by, all asking the same question that Lisa had asked: "Why was I here on my day off?"

When Lisa came out, she said: "You're surely not here because of that newspaper article, are you?"

"Well, as a matter of fact, I am," I said. "I was worried that everyone would be as upset as I was."

"Jean was quite upset," said Lisa. "She's talked with a few residents and a few families, but everything seems to be O.K.."

"Is she still here?" I asked.

"I'm not sure," said Lisa. "You can check her office. You know, you might have a little talk with Charlotte Danner. She was the most upset."

"I don't know what to say," I said. "I really can't say everything is O.K., if we don't know."

"Just let her do the talking," advised Lisa.

I thought I'd check to see if Jean was in her office before I went down to see Mrs. Danner, since I didn't know how long Jean would stay. I peered into her office. Jean was sitting hunched over the desk. When I knocked, she turned around and I saw that she'd been crying.

"Oh, Jean, are you alright?" I asked. She just shook her head. I walked over and took the seat beside her desk.

"Can I get you something?" I asked.

"Maybe a cold washcloth," she said. I walked out to the unit to find one and brought it back with a glass of water. I handed these to her and sat down again, but didn't say anything.

"You know we work so hard to give good care," she said with tears starting to well up in her eyes again. "And then something like this happens. How could they write such awful things about us? Who's behind this?"

I reached out to touch Jean's arm. What could I say?

"I know someone is stealing, but I don't believe that anyone is harming our residents," she continued. "Do you?"

"I don't know, Jean," I answered. "It's hard to believe."

"I've been trying to reassure people all morning, Nora," she said, "but the truth of the matter is, if we can't figure out what's going on, we may have to close."

"You mean, close 2 West? Or close Marian Manor?" I asked. "And why?"

"We cannot put people at risk," she said. "It's purely and simply that."

"Well, we're not closing today," I said. "You need to go home and get some rest. We need you to be strong. Lisa says that everyone out there is doing fine. She just asked me to check on Mrs. Danner."

"Oh, Mrs. Danner. I wanted to check on her myself," said Jean. "She's been so depressed since the death of June Michaels, but she wasn't in her room when I checked earlier." She paused, dabbing her eyes with a tissue. "You're probably right. I'll go home. Tomorrow will be better!"

At that, there was a knock on the door and Dan appeared in the doorway. "Hi, Jean," he said. "Are you about ready to go, Nora?"

"Give me another minute," I said to Dan, watching Jean's eyebrows go up. "It's not what you think," I said to Jean quickly. Dan had closed the door. "We just happened to be playing golf at the same time, with some friends. He offered to give me a ride over here when we saw the headlines." Jean was nodding her head and trying to suppress a smile. "He wanted to check things out for himself. He did." I could see that Jean was struggling to hold back her laughter.

"Oh Nora, you're always so serious about everything," she said. "What's wrong with someone thinking you might be seeing Detective Maguire?"

"Nothing's wrong with it," I fumed. "It's just not so." At that, I got up and left Jean's office, calling back: "Get some rest. I'll see you on Monday."

I could hear her laughing softly as I walked out, but I wasn't going to give her any more ammunition. Anyway, it was good she was laughing. I signaled to Dan that I needed one more minute. He was waiting patiently by the desk, reading the bulletin board. As I walked towards Mrs. Danner's room, I stopped to chat with several residents. Clark Skinner made a point of drawing me off to one side.

"I just wanted to tell you, Nora, that I think it was wrong of Dr. Graves to criticize you in front of me yesterday afternoon," he said. "I like Dr. Graves, but I think she was out of line. You're an excellent nurse, or will be, and I would say that to anyone." I thanked Mr. Skinner and gave him a hug. This was why I was going to be a nurse.

When I reached Mrs. Danner's room, I saw she was stretched out on the bed, with her hands folded across her chest. I walked over and touched her hands lightly. She didn't move. It occurred to me that her hands felt a bit chilly. I looked again. Charlotte Danner was not breathing and when I checked, I couldn't feel a pulse. I ran to the door, grabbed the emergency facemask and yelled for "help." Then I ran back to Mrs. Danner, pulled the headboard off the bed, turned her on her side and slid the board under her back. I began CPR. Cardiopulmonary Resuscitation.

I don't remember exactly what happened next, but lots of people came into the room. One of the nurses helped me with CPR and another nurse set up the AED (Automatic External Defibrillator). Someone had called "911" and the paramedics were there to take over within minutes. They managed to revive Mrs. Danner and then they transported her to Harrison Hospital. There were a lot of people with a lot of questions, but Jean and Lisa seemed to be handling everything.

Dan took my elbow and guided me through the group of people at the nurses' station and he didn't release his grip until we were back to his truck. Once we were in the truck, he said: "I think it's time we had a little talk."

"About what?" I asked innocently, looking him straight in the eye.

"About Marian Manor. About what's been happening to your residents," said Dan. "I just feel that you know more than you're letting on."

"That's not true," I said.

"Nobody gets this involved unless they know something, or think they know something," said Dan. "My gut tells me that you know something that I don't know."

"I don't know anything," I said. "I had some ideas, but they didn't pan out."

"Well, let's talk about those ideas," said Dan. He started the truck.

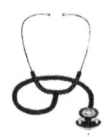

Chapter 12

On the way back to the golf course, I gave Dan a brief rundown on what I knew, which was to say, nothing. I told him about my initial suspicions and how I'd tried to correlate the work schedules with what had happened.

"I know you've been trying to help," said Dan.

"I hear a 'but' coming," I said. What I really heard coming was a lecture.

"The 'but' is that you need to let the police do its job and you need to concentrate on doing yours," said Dan. "Do you think a murderer, if that's what we're dealing with, is going to like having you on his tail? Do you think he'll hesitate to kill again to protect himself?"

"I didn't think about that part," I said. I felt pretty stupid. I was also annoyed that he had the nerve to tell me to do my job.

"I probably shouldn't do this, but let me give you a few other things to think about," said Dan, "maybe over a cup of coffee?"

Curiosity outweighed my unwillingness to hear another lecture, so I agreed to the coffee. I picked up my car and followed Dan over to the marina. Once we were settled in a booth and the coffee was served, he continued.

"You have to look at the bigger picture, Nora," he began. "First of all, the thefts have involved some pretty pricey items. The thief has to be able to cash them in somewhere and that would be impossible in a small town like this. He either takes them to a bigger town himself, or he has a contact that will do this for him. If we're looking at murder, well, that's something else. And, remember, we still don't have the final reports from the coroner."

Dan paused, apparently waiting for me to comment. When I didn't say anything, he shrugged and continued. I was actually enjoying this. I had a lot to learn.

"Surely you've read enough mysteries to know that there are three elements in every crime: motive, means and opportunity. There has to be a reason. There has to be some way to do it, and there has to be the chance to do it."

"So, what you're saying is that I have been concentrating on who had the 'opportunity' without really considering the 'why' or 'how,' is that it?" I asked.

"Exactly," said Dan. "Since I can't see you dropping this matter, maybe we can work together. What do you think?"

"I don't know, Dan, could I think about it?" I asked.

"What's to think about?" asked Dan.

"I don't want anyone at work to think I'm a snitch," I said.

"Just let them think you and I are dating," said Dan. "No one would question your contact with me then."

"They might question my taste," I said, smiling.

"That's a low blow," said Dan, also smiling.

"O.K., it's a good plan," I said. "Where do we start?"

"Do you still have those schedules?" asked Dan.

"I have them at home," I said. "Oh, wait a minute, at Deborah's house." I explained the problem with my apartment.

"Well, let's look at those again," said Dan. "You had a good idea, but maybe two heads are better than one."

We drove over to Deborah's and I spread the schedules on the kitchen table. I showed Dan the chart I had made. He had many of the same questions I had asked myself. I gave him the same answers. "What about the Claytons?" he asked.

"I don't think Sam is capable of doing anything dishonest," I said, "but I'm not sure about Iris." I told him about the conversation I had overheard and about mention of the "Allen account."

"What do you know about the Claytons?" asked Dan.

"Well, Sam has lived in Jacobsport all his life," I said. "He married Iris shortly after they both graduated from Del Norte State. He studied business and then went on to get his nursing home administrator's license. Sam's mother was a nurse. She was very caring and did a lot to help senior citizens in this town. Marian Manor is named for her."

"What about Iris?" asked Dan.

"I'm not sure what Iris studied," I said. "She thinks of herself as an artist, but I've never seen any of her work. She likes expensive clothes and she drives a Lexus."

"Do you think Iris is capable of stealing from, or harming a resident?" asked Dan.

"I don't know," I answered truthfully.

"Well, let's look at the three elements. Iris apparently had some financial concerns. That would give her a motive, right?" he asked.

"Right," I answered.

"And she can go anywhere that she wants to go in the building, right?" he asked.

"Right," I answered again.

"Including a resident's room? Whether the resident is in or not, correct?" he asked.

"Correct," I answered.

"That gives her the means," he said. "She also has a car and the money to leave the area if she so desires."

"I see where you're going," I said. "What about opportunity?"

"Well, didn't you say that either she or Sam visit each unit daily and that they often stop and talk with both residents and staff?" he asked.

"O.K., so she has the opportunity on a daily basis, right?" I asked.

"Right," said Dan.

"It seems too easy," I said. "I just feel we're missing something here."

"O.K. Let's see if these same three elements will fit anyone else," he suggested.

We played with that idea for a while, but since we really didn't know much about anyone else's finances, we were stuck. You could say that almost anyone who worked in a nursing home didn't make much money and therefore could be looking to make some on the side. Then you could say that almost everyone who worked at Marian Manor had the means and the opportunity to commit the crimes. This was giving me another headache and we were no closer to solving anything. I said this to Dan.

"But we are closer, Nora," he said. "We've studied a number of possibilities. That's what you have to do."

"Maybe we should be thinking in a totally different direction," I said.

"What do you mean?" asked Dan.

"I don't know for sure," I said, "but, maybe, it isn't just one person. Maybe there are several people involved."

"Good, Nora," he said, "thinking outside the box!"

We spent another hour looking at all the staff again. We tried to figure out who might be friends. Who might need money. Who was dressing better, or driving a better car than they should be able to afford. We still came up empty, mostly because I didn't know the staff very well. It looked like it was time for a break.

"I'd like to go back to the hospital to see how Mrs. Danner is doing," I said. "I also need to check on Stella, my landlady. She's supposed to be coming over to Marian Manor tomorrow."

"That's a good idea," said Dan. "I'd also like to know what they found on Mrs. Danner. Maybe we can get more information, if I'm with you."

"I'll take my own car this time because I have to go and feed Eugene afterwards," I said. I explained who Eugene was.

"No problem," said Dan. "I have other stops to make too. I just want to say thanks for all your help." He pulled a business card from his pocket and handed it to me. "In case I didn't give you this before, here's my card. Call me anytime if you think of something else."

"You mean we don't have to schedule a 'date'?" I asked with a straight face.

"What do you mean?" asked Dan.

"Well I thought you were going to protect my reputation with the staff by letting them think we're dating," I said. "How quickly one forgets!" I could see Dan's face was turning a bright red, so I hurried us out the door.

When Dan and I got to Harrison Hospital, we went in through the emergency room entrance. Dan flashed his badge and asked to speak to the nurse in charge. When the nurse came, we introduced ourselves and asked for an update on Mrs. Danner. The nurse explained that she couldn't discuss Mrs. Danner's condition because of confidentiality issues. She did tell us that Mrs. Danner had been admitted to the telemetry unit for some additional tests. This told me that the doctors probably thought it was a problem with Mrs. Danner's heart. Telemetry is one way to monitor a patient's heart. The patient wears a small radio-like device where they can still get up and walk around.

We thanked the nurse and headed upstairs. Mrs. Danner was sitting up in bed and dozing. I walked in, stood beside the bed and placed my hand on top of hers. Dan stood in the doorway, apparently waiting to see if Mrs. Danner was awake.

Mrs. Danner opened her eyes and smiled. "Oh Nora, I'm so glad that you're here," she said. "They tell me you saved my life. Thank you so much."

"Mrs. Danner, I'm glad to see you're O.K.," I said. "Do you remember anything?"

"I just remember trying to get a sweater off the closet shelf and I felt dizzy," she said. "I just wanted to lie down. I guess that's when my heart stopped. I don't remember anything else until I woke up in the emergency room."

"You remember Detective Maguire," I said, indicating Dan who was still in the doorway. "He also wanted to make sure you were alright. We're going to let you rest now." Mrs. Danner nodded to Dan.

"I am tired," she said, closing her eyes. I patted her hand.

As we walked down the hall, Dan and I each heaved a sigh of relief. "At least this time there doesn't seem to be any foul play," I said.

"Lucky for her," said Dan, shrugging his shoulder towards Mrs. Danner's room. "O.K., I'm taking off." As he turned to walk away, he changed his mind and came back. He hesitated. "Nora ... Did you ever take care of Harriet Allen? On 2 East?"

"Yes," I replied, startled by his change of direction. "Why? You did ask me this before, you know."

"What can you tell me about her?" he asked, not answering my question.

"I didn't know her very well, but I liked her," I replied. "She was a very bright lady with a nice family."

"A family that doesn't think too much of Marian Manor," said Dan, more to himself than to me. "Anyway, enjoy the rest of the weekend and I'll talk with you next week."

"Dan, wait," I said, but he was already halfway down the hall. What was that all about? What did Harriet Allen have to do with anything??

After Dan left, I continued down the hall to Stella's room. She was putting on a beautiful, red kimono that I had seen her wear at home. She had bought it on one of her many trips to Asia.

"And just where do you think you're going, all dressed up like this?" I asked.

"Oh, Nora, it's so good to see you," said Stella. "I was beginning to think you weren't coming today."

"I was playing golf this morning and then I had some other stops to make," I explained. "It's been a busy day." I wasn't going to bring up the newspaper article. If Stella had read it, she didn't seem concerned.

"Well, you probably know I'm going to Marian Manor tomorrow," she said. "I know I have some things to learn before I go home." She emphasized that last part.

"I'm looking forward to seeing you there," I said. "I know we can help you get ready to go home. Eugene misses you."

"And I miss him," said Stella. "Does Marian Manor let you have pets?"

"No, but we do let them come to visit you," I said. "How about a walk down the hall before your dinner?"

"I can see you're going to be a slave driver," said Stella. "O.K. A short one." She straightened herself up, steadied herself with the walker and started towards the door.

"Did the therapist O.K. you walking with those slippers?" I asked, noticing the silk embroidered slippers that matched her kimono.

"He didn't see them," she answered quickly.

"Stella, you can't walk in those," I said. "They're too slippery. They're beautiful, but they're not safe. You could fall very easily and you don't want that after just having had surgery. You need your walking shoes for support."

"But I can't wear those monstrous things," she protested. "They don't go with my kimono."

"You'll be in perfect style, Stella," I countered. "Haven't you seen any fashion magazines lately? Women are wearing dressy clothes with combat boots!" O.K., maybe not 90-year-old women. Still.

"Yes, I know, but it's not my style," she pouted, turning her walker back into the room. I got out her walking shoes and helped her put them on. When we walked down the hall, everyone complimented her on her beautiful kimono. Each time she lamented the fact that she couldn't wear the matching slippers.

When Stella was settled back in her room, I said good-by and left, saying that I would check on her at Marian Manor on Sunday afternoon. I then stopped by Mrs. Danner's room again, but she was still dozing. I didn't disturb her.

Driving back to Deborah's after having stopped to feed Eugene, I thought over all that had happened. I had enjoyed playing golf with the guys. The residents and staff seemed to be doing O.K. despite the newspaper article. Mrs. Danner was O.K. Stella seemed settled on the question of coming to Marian Manor and working with Dan wasn't so bad. But we still didn't have any answers!

Chapter 13

Monday morning. We were waiting for report.

"So, Tina, how was your weekend?" I asked, pulling my chair up to hers. "You look a bit tired. Ready for the marathon?" She had been training with friends.

"I'm tired, but the weekend was great!" said Tina, giving me a sly look. "Understand we had a little excitement here on Saturday, Nora. Sounds like you saved Mrs. Danner's life. You've impressed everyone!"

"All in a day's work," I replied, fiddling with my clipboard and avoiding her eyes. I knew what was coming next.

"And what's this I hear about you and Detective Maguire?" she continued.

"What did you hear?" I asked.

"Only that you two were here together," replied Tina. "Good for you!"

"It's not what it looked like," I said. "Jimmy set up this foursome for Saturday. I didn't even know who else was playing. When we saw that newspaper headline, Detective Maguire and I both wanted to come over here. That's all there was to it."

"Nothing more, huh?" asked Tina, eyebrows elevated.

"Nothing more," I said, anxious to move on to something else. "Tell me more about your weekend?"

"Well, there were six of us who have done this before," said Tina. "We're all running next weekend. We ran. We swam and we cycled. It was fun, but I'm beat."

"Well, I hope your day isn't too bad," I said. "Did you hear that Stella moved in here yesterday?"

"I heard," Tina replied. "How's she doing?"

"I haven't seen her this morning," I said, "but I'm sure she'll do fine."

It was a busy morning. There were the usual meds, dressings and treatments. Several doctors stopped in, including Dr. Graves who made a point of saying hello. That was strange. Then I went down to the Activities room to see what was happening downstairs. There I met the "three amigos," as the Mr.'s Parker, Jessel and Lowenstein had come to be called.

Mr. Parker was thrilled to be learning so much about the computer. "Let me show you what I found today," he said, sitting down at the monitor. Mr. Jessel and Mr. Lowenstein rolled their eyes.

"I have to check with Kathy about something," I said. "You guys go ahead."

"Lucky you," said Mr. Jessel, smiling. Mr. Parker looked up at Mr. Jessel with a question on his face. He obviously hadn't heard the remark. Mr. Jessel patted him on the back.

The Activities Room was a big cheery place on the first floor. The three amigos were gathered around one of the two computer terminals in one corner. The owner of a local yarn shop was teaching a knitting class in one corner and I saw Kathy, the Activities Director, in a third corner doing what looked like the preparations for another project. She was cutting pieces of green felt from a large bolt sitting on the countertop. "What are you working on, Kathy?" I asked.

"I'm re-doing our bulletin boards," she replied. "I don't know what I'm doing, but you can never have too many leaves!" The bulletin boards were hung on each unit and in the dining rooms. They highlighted upcoming activities, menus and the accomplishments of the residents.

"How are you and Mr. Parker doing with your Internet search?" I asked. "He talks about nothing else."

"Nora, you won't believe this, and I'm not positive, but it looks like Mr. Parker and Mr. Jessel might actually be twins!" she exclaimed. "We haven't told anyone yet and you can't either. We need to check a few more things."

"It wouldn't surprise me," I said. "They look so much alike and have so many of the same interests."

"But, did you know, they have the same birthday?" asked Kathy. "I just found that out myself."

"Wow," I said. "I had forgotten that."

"Record keeping was so different in those days," said Kathy. "Only a DNA test will tell us for sure." A DNA test is done with a sample of blood or skin, or some body fluid from one person, which can be compared with a sample from another person. Each sample is unique for each person, but there will be certain things in common if people are related to one another. It can be an expensive test.

"What does Mr. Parker say?" I asked.

"I don't think it's sunk in yet," said Kathy. "He knows they were born the same day. He also knows there were two baby boys born on that day right here at Harrison Hospital, but the names are different. He knows we've started a search to see if there were any other boys born on that day, in any other hospital within a hundred miles. A hundred miles is stretching what would have been a reasonable distance to travel in those days."

"Has he said anything to Mr. Jessel?" I asked.

"He didn't want to say anything until we knew more," said Kathy. "One big problem for us is that most children were born at home in those days. Oftentimes, the births were never recorded.

If they were recorded, it could have been days later, so accuracy can be a big problem."

"So now what do you do?" I asked.

"Well, I'm going to talk with Sam Clayton, or maybe Dr. McCain, to see what they think," said Kathy. "These guys don't have money for DNA testing, so I want to see if we can help with this."

"This is really exciting, Kathy," I said. "I promise not to say anything until you're ready." I turned to leave. "Thanks for the update."

"Anytime, Nora," said Kathy. "We have the high school choir coming in this afternoon. Come down and join us."

"I'm not sure how the afternoon looks, but I'll try," I said. "Thanks again."

I started to go back upstairs, but then decided to see how Stella was doing with her first therapy session. When I looked in, she and Tony, the physical therapist, were deep in conversation while he had her doing some leg exercises. I decided not to interrupt.

Back upstairs, it was time for lunch. I helped the aides get residents up and ready for lunch. I passed the few meds that were scheduled and then I helped feed a few residents who were unable to feed themselves. I always enjoyed this quiet time when I could just sit with a resident. There is a great sense of accomplishment when I can get someone to eat or drink, especially if this has been difficult.

After the residents finished lunch, it was my turn. Usually I brought my lunch, but since I had been staying with Deborah, it was easier to eat in the staff dining room. When I walked into the dining room, it was empty. Most staff liked to eat early, to be sure they got what they wanted. I decided to have the special of the day, a homemade chicken potpie and a salad. The food here was usually pretty good, but I could save some money if I brought my own from home.

After picking up a drink, I chose a table over by the window and pulled out my book. I always carry a book in case I have to wait on something. Today I was reading an old Stephen King I had picked up at a second hand bookstore.

I was just getting into the chapter when I heard: "Hey, Nora, glad to find you." It was Dan, carrying a lunch tray. This was a surprise. "Mind if I sit down."

"Hi, Dan," I said, closing my book. "Have a seat. Didn't expect to see you so soon."

"Well, I got the reports from Jimmy today and I wanted to update the staff," he said. "I've spoken with Sam and Jean. And … since I did suggest we work together, I thought you would want to know. Melba Jones died of natural causes. She had another stroke."

"Thanks, Dan," I said. "But, what was that you mentioned about Harriet Allen the other day?" I asked. "Is she part of this?"

"Unfortunately, we're never going to know about Harriet Allen," said Dan. "She was cremated before anyone realized there may have been foul play."

"What makes you think there may have been foul play?" I asked.

"Her family," said Dan. "Apparently, Mrs. Allen made a substantial contribution to Marian Manor before her death. No one knew this until the reading of the will."

"Wow," I said. "That's probably what Sam and Iris were talking about!"

"Maybe," said Dan.

"And June Michaels?" I asked

"Well, understand that this is confidential," said Dan, leaning in, "but it appears that Mrs. Michaels might have been given an overdose—one of her heart medicines. The final report isn't in."

"Then, that would mean she was murdered?" I asked.

"Yes, but we can't jump to that conclusion just yet," he said. "From what I understand, it's possible for some medicines to build up in the blood and become toxic. The liver and kidneys don't work as well in older people. If that's the case here, then it wouldn't be murder."

"I'd much rather believe that," I said. "I hate to think anyone here would kill someone. It's hard enough to believe we have a thief in our midst."

"I agree," said Dan. "So let's wait for that final report."

When we finished lunch, I still had time before I was due back on the unit. I offered to give Dan a quick tour of the Marian Manor grounds. As we rounded the right side of the building and went towards the back, we saw two people standing by a sleek black car. A black Lexus. Iris Clayton's car.

"Who's that with Iris Clayton?" asked Dan.

"That's Dominic," I replied. "Dominic Angelini. You met him. He's one of our nurses' aides."

"Are he and Iris friends?" asked Dan.

"I wasn't aware of it, if they are," I said.

"Well it certainly looks like they're having quite a conversation now," said Dan, as we watched the two. They were leaning over the hood of the car with their heads together. Dominic looked up. When he saw us, he said something to Iris. She turned to look at us, while starting to fold up whatever they had been looking at. As we continued walking towards them, Dominic said something else to Iris and then began walking towards the back door. Iris got into her car, started it up and drove off.

"Wouldn't you like to know what that was all about?" asked Dan.

"There's nothing wrong with them talking to each other," I said.

"And what exactly do you think those two have in common?" asked Dan.

"I don't know," I said, "but I think we should be able to talk with whomever we want." I knew exactly what Dan meant and I knew I was being argumentative, but I was unwilling to think badly of Dominic.

"So you're telling me you see nothing odd about this?" asked Dan.

"O.K.," I answered slowly. "I do think it's odd. I don't know what they would have in common, but I think we should try to find out."

"That's more like it," said Dan. "Why don't you see what you can find out about Dominic and I'll work on Iris."

"But Dominic is a friend," I said. "I work with him everyday. We're partners."

"Do you want to find out what's going on in this place?" asked Dan, somewhat exasperated. He gave me time to think, and then said, "You'll have to ruffle a few feathers, Nora. My guess is you don't mind ruffling feathers."

"O.K.," I said. "You're right. I'll see what I can find out."

"Call me when you get something," said Dan.

"And you call me, if you get something," I reminded him.

"You've got it," said Dan.

We walked back to the front parking area. Dan drove off in his unmarked, non-descript, white police car. It fit. I thought about my first impression of Dan, that everything about him was average. Maybe he wasn't so average.

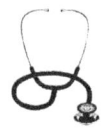

Chapter 14

When I got back to the unit after lunch, I was still mulling over my conversation with Dan. I sat doing some charting, when suddenly I remembered our conversation from Saturday. What if there was more than one person involved? They didn't have to be friends, did they? What if Iris and Dominic were the thieves? How did they manage it? Would either of them be capable of murder?

Tina interrupted my train of thought. "That Stella, is a real character!" she said, sitting down at the desk. "I love her."

"She is a character," I agreed.

"The stories she can tell!" said Tina. "I could stay in her room all day."

"What did she tell you?" I asked.

"About her trips to Asia. When she was with the ballet," Tina replied. "I love that red kimono."

"I hope she's not wearing those matching slippers," I said.

"No, she wanted to wear them," said Tina, "but Tony gave her the lecture about how unsafe they were."

"Good," I said.

"So. I heard you had lunch with Detective Maguire," said Tina. "What's that all about?"

"Who told you?" I asked.

"Well, Dominic for one," said Tina. "He saw you two walking out back."

"He wanted the outside tour," I said. "That's all."

"You know, Nora, he's kind of cute," said Tina.

I gave Tina a long look. "It's strictly professional," I said.

"Nora, I'm just teasing," said Tina, smiling. Then she changed the subject. "When do you get back into your apartment?"

"Hopefully tomorrow or the next day," I said. "I can't wait. Not that Deborah hasn't been great, but I just want my own space."

As we sat there talking, Jean joined us. She asked if I would like to have another weekend off. Lisa wanted to work and they didn't need the extra staff. "Sure," I said. "But that means I'll have to work Thursday. I have to have the hours for school."

"That's fine," said Jean. "I'll let Lisa know."

Suddenly, there was a piercing scream from down the hall. It sounded like Stella. The three of us ran towards her room. "What's the matter, Stella?" I asked. She was sitting up in her wheelchair with the drawer of the bedside table in her lap. The contents were strewn across the bed.

"It's my diamond earrings," said Stella. "They're gone."

"Are you sure that Pamela didn't take them with her?" I asked.

"No," said Stella emphatically. "She wanted to, but I insisted she leave them here with me."

"Are you sure they were in the bedside table?" asked Tina. "Maybe someone put them in your closet." She walked over to the closet and started sorting through the pockets of Stella's clothes.

"I want the police called now," said Stella. "No one gets away with stealing my things. You know I didn't want to come here, Nora. Now look what's happened." She started to cry.

I sat with Stella, trying to calm her down. When that didn't work, Tina went to see if there was a medicine that would help Stella relax. Jean went to call Sam Clayton, who would undoubtedly notify the police. Tina came back with a small pill that Stella took readily. I stayed with her until the medicine took effect and Stella relaxed.

As I was setting up my afternoon meds, Dominic came down the hall, smiling. "So Dominic, I understand you're spreading gossip about me," I said.

"What do you mean?" he laughed.

"You know what I mean," I said. Then I took a bold step. "And just what were you and Iris up to out there?"

Dominic hesitated for only a second, but it was enough to tell me he was on guard. "Tara and I are going to San Francisco this weekend," he replied. "I happened to mention this when Iris was around and she had some suggestions. That's all. She was showing me some places on the map."

"You and Tara?" I asked.

"O.K., I know we haven't advertised our relationship," said Dominic, with a flush creeping up from his neckline, "but we've been dating for a while."

"So where are you going?" I asked.

"We haven't decided yet, but probably most of the usual tourist places," he replied. "Fisherman's Wharf, Ghirardelli Square, Golden Gate Park, the art museums—you know."

"Sounds like fun," I said, not really sure if I believed him. "Anyway, how is everyone doing up here?" I asked, getting back to our day's assignment. He assured me everyone was doing fine except for several residents who had requested pain meds. I made a note to give those meds first.

After I finished the afternoon meds and treatments, I sat down again to chart. When I looked up, there was Dan. "This is getting to be your second home, Detective Maguire," I said.

"Well, I'll know my way around when it's my turn to be a resident," he said. "I need to talk with Jean. You probably know why I'm here."

"I know. Stella's really upset," I said. "Just a minute, I'll go find Jean." I found her in the utility room, discussing cleaning problems with Maggie, the housekeeper. "Detective Maguire is here," I said.

"Tell him I'll be right out," said Jean.

I let Dan know about Jean and then I filled him in on my conversation with Dominic. "What do you think?" he asked.

"I don't know." I answered. "It's possible they'll just be sightseeing, but my gut tells me there's more to the story."

"Trust your gut," said Dan. "What about Stella's earrings?"

"I think someone took a big risk, in light of all that happened over the weekend," I said. "Maybe it's a false alarm. I don't know."

"It could also be that this person thinks he's smarter than everyone else, that he'll never be caught," said Dan. "What do you mean by a false alarm?"

"Well Stella has been pretty forgetful lately," I said. "I didn't talk with her daughter Pamela yet. I thought you would probably do that. Maybe Pamela took the earrings home for safekeeping."

"Thanks for letting the police do their job," he said with a smile.

Jean arrived and led Dan into her office. They didn't stay long, but by the time they finished, it was time to give report to the evening staff. I went down to check on Stella. She was dozing so I didn't wake her. I didn't know if Stella had talked with Dan, or if Dan had talked with Pamela. I did see Dan out in the hall, talking with Tina. When I left the building, there was a police officer at the door, checking belongings. That seemed kind of pointless as whoever took the earrings could have stashed them anywhere. I didn't say this, however. I let the police do their thing.

After leaving Marian Manor, I stopped by to feed Eugene, ran some errands and grabbed a sandwich with my friend Mary. By the time I got to Deborah's, it was late and she had just gotten home.

"How was your trip?" I asked.

"I had a great time," said Deborah. "They had so much going

on for the families, but Rose and Jane had their own ideas about what we should do. It was exhausting."

"Well, get a good night's sleep," I said, "because things have been hopping at work." I gave her a quick rundown on the excitement we'd been having.

As I lay in bed that night, I thought again about my conversation with Dominic. Something didn't ring true. I thought it was nice that Dominic and Tara were dating. Maybe they were just going to San Francisco for fun. But what if they were the link between the thief and the money? What if they were going to sell the stolen jewelry? I wished I could be invisible and follow them to the city. Suddenly, I felt the seed of a plan beginning to grow in my mind. Maybe I would take a trip to San Francisco myself.

It was good I only talked with Dan once more during the rest of the week. He had stopped by for another staff meeting where he officially announced that the death of Melba Jones was from natural causes and that the results on June Michaels' death were still pending. I didn't want him to know I planned on going to San Francisco this weekend. I didn't tell anyone, except Pamela Ward who would need to take care of Eugene. I only told her I was going to be "away."

I moved back to my own apartment during the week and I was thrilled. There really was "no place like home." While my apartment was always quiet, it was even more so now with Stella being gone. I wasn't sure if I liked that part or not. It was, however, a lot easier taking care of Eugene.

Tina was focused on the marathon and didn't question my not going. I used the excuse that I had to get re-settled in my apartment. A number of our friends from school would be there to cheer her on. I called family friends in San Francisco who were happy to put me up for a few nights. I had no idea what I was going to do once I got there, but I knew I had to try to find out what, if anything, Dominic and Iris were up to.

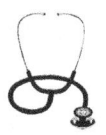

Chapter 15

Saturday morning I was on the road by 5:30. I loved the drive down to San Francisco through the redwoods. It was always beautiful. With the music cranked up, the six-hour drive was nothing for my little Mazda. It had 150,000 miles on it, but it drove as well as it did when I first got it. My friends told me it was time for a new car, but that would have to wait until after graduation. And I didn't know if I could ever part with this one.

While driving, I tried to figure out how I would find Dominic and Tara. I knew where they were supposed to be going, but where should I start? How would I find them among all the other tourists? If I did find them, I had to figure out how to follow them without being seen. There was just the ghost of a thought that maybe I shouldn't do this. Maybe it was Iris who should have been followed, or maybe the whole thing was a wild goose chase. My gut told me to follow Dominic. Dan had told me to follow my gut. That was one good thing.

I decided to start with Ghiradelli Square, known for its wonderful chocolate and interesting shops. I would find one of those nice coffee shops, with outside seating and an understanding waiter. If I stayed in one place, it seemed more likely that I would see Dominic and Tara come by. I had to hope they would come by.

Most people who go to San Francisco visit Fisherman's Wharf and Ghiradelli's is just across from this. Everyone ends up there, if not for the chocolate, then to visit one of the many little restaurants or shops. It was also the end of the cable car line and every tourist had to ride the cable car at least once.

It was lunchtime when I got to Ghiradelli's. I found a coffee shop with sandwiches and outside seating. I ordered some lunch and sat back in a corner. This allowed me to get a good look at people passing from all directions. I had a floppy hat, sunglasses and a newspaper to duck behind if necessary. The table I chose had an umbrella to shade me, but it was a beautiful day to be outside.

By 2:30 I hadn't seen Dominic and Tara. I was beginning to think how really stupid my idea had been. While the waiter hadn't said anything, I was also beginning to feel uncomfortable taking up a table even though the shop didn't seem to be that busy. I signaled the waiter and ordered a latte to go. I explained that I was still waiting for someone who must have gotten lost in traffic. The waiter seemed to accept this and assured me there was no hurry. Waiters probably heard this excuse a lot.

At 3:30 I was still sitting in the same spot. I was restless, but unwilling to give up. My latte was cold. I was now completely convinced of my stupidity. Just as I was thinking about leaving, I spotted them. Dominic and Tara were walking up from Fisherman's Wharf. They were talking and laughing and didn't seem to be aware of anyone other than each other. They were headed towards Ghiradelli's. I quickly paid my bill and looked around for another shop where I could watch them without being noticed.

I didn't see a shop with a good view, so I chose one of the outside benches that had some large plants around it. I knew I was going to be there for a while because the lines at Ghiradelli's take forever. It was then that I wondered if maybe I was already too late. What if Dominic and Tara, if they were the thieves, had already unloaded the stolen jewelry? What if now they were just enjoying their time in the city?

Suddenly, the two were almost on top of me. Apparently they had decided not to wait in line at Ghiradelli's. I ducked behind my newspaper.

"C'mon, Tara," said Dominic. "I want to get to Chinatown." He was guiding Tara by her elbow.

"We've got plenty of time," said Tara. "Just let me pick up a few souvenirs."

Dominic shrugged. "O.K., O.K.," he said, "but you know we'll have to wait for the cable car."

"I know," said Tara. "I'll be quick, but there's so much to see."

As they passed, I got up and followed their voices, trying to keep my head down and my back to them as much as possible. While Tara was browsing in one shop, Dominic pulled his cell from a pocket and made a call. I looked for a way to get closer so I could hear what he said. Just then, three little old ladies passed by me, going towards the shop. I hunched over a bit and joined them, separating myself just before they got to Dominic. I straightened up and walked into the shop next door. I lingered in the shop's doorway.

"I know I told you we would be there by 3:00, but we had some things to do," said Dominic. "Yes, we have the stuff. We're going to catch the cable car as soon as we can. We'll be there." He flicked his cell closed, impatiently. "Tara, c'mon, we're late." For the first time I noticed that Dominic was carrying a small black satchel.

I debated about whether I should go ahead of them, or stay behind them. I decided I probably should go on ahead. If the lines were long to get on the cable car, as they often were on weekends, I may not make it on the same car they did. It was a risk if they recognized me, but they wouldn't be looking for anyone from Jacobsport. It may not click with them, even if they did see my face.

I started walking towards the cable car stop at the foot of Hyde Street. The lines didn't seem too bad. I had to pace myself so I wouldn't be too far ahead of Dominic and Tara. Looking back at them, I began to wonder what exactly I was going to do if Dominic had the stolen property, or if he tried to sell it. I realized there were a lot of things I should have thought about before I made this trip.

I got in line for the cable car, trying to space myself so I would be in the same group as Dominic and Tara. I kept my back to them as much as I could and tried to appear like I was with a group of tourists from Ohio. When my turn came to get in the car, I chose a spot on the outside, at the back, so I could get off quickly if Dominic and Tara did. For the moment there was nothing to do but enjoy the ride.

As the car began the steep ascent up Hyde Street, amid all the "oohs" and "aahs" of the tourists, I saw Dominic and Tara looking back at the bay. They were smiling and enjoying the ride. At the top of the hill, the car took a left on Washington as it worked its way towards Chinatown. After a few more turns and before I knew what was happening, Dominic and Tara jumped off. Watching them walk away, I was frustrated and I quickly pulled the cord for the next stop. I knew it was better if we didn't get off at the same time. With few people on these streets, I would have been spotted immediately. But now to find them!

The next stop put me several blocks from where Dominic and Tara had gotten off. I had to double back, which meant walking uphill on California, which is very steep. I took a left at the second street and saw Dominic and Tara about a block ahead of me, walking slowly past the old apartment buildings. After another block, they turned left again into a spooky street of abandoned shops. There were cobwebbed windows, large black metal gates and faded names over the trash-strewn doorways. Just when I thought everything was closed, I saw Dominic and Tara cross the street and walk into a shop on the far side. The faded gold sign above the shop said "Tommy's Pawn Shop." In the window was a red neon sign flashing "Buy—Sell—Loan."

Since I couldn't actually follow them into the shop, I decided to walk past it as if I were intent on getting someplace else. I knew I was taking a chance, but I figured if they were unloading the stolen jewelry, it would take them a while to make a deal. As I walked by I saw Dominic and Tara at the counter and who should be with them, but Iris! I could also see that Dominic was holding up, what looked like June Michaels' letter opener. I had to force myself to keep walking. I had to think this through and I needed help. There was only one person to call.

After walking another block, I found a bench and sat down. I could still see the pawn shop. I pulled out my cell, found Dan's number and hit "send." To my surprise he answered immediately. "Hi, Dan," I said. "Guess where I am."

"Nora?" he replied. "What's up?"

"You're not going to like this," I said. "I'm in San Francisco." I heard a groan on the other end. "I've been following Dominic and Tara, but here's the good part. They're in a pawn shop and guess who's with them?"

"I'm not really into games," said Dan tightly. "What's going on?"

This was not fun. "Well, Iris is with them," I said, "and I think I saw June Michaels' letter opener."

"Where are you, Nora?" asked Dan.

"I told you," I replied. "I'm in San Francisco."

"I mean where in San Francisco?" asked Dan, in a voice usually reserved for small children.

I looked around for street signs. "Emerald and Acacia," I replied.

"Stay put," said Dan. "I'll call San Francisco P.D. What's your cell number?"

"226-3422," I replied.

I'll call you back," he said. He did. "The police are on their way. Stay where you are until they arrive."

I tried to do this, but as I watched the shop, I saw the trio coming out the door of the shop. They were leaving. I had a choice: let them see me and keep them talking until the police arrived, or take the chance they would leave before the police arrived. I shouted "hi" and ran towards them.

As I did this, I saw surprise, confusion, worry and then anger on their faces. "Nora, what are you doing here?" asked Iris, heatedly when I reached them.

"I could ask you the same thing," I said, lightly. "What are you doing at a pawn shop?" I knew I really had no right to ask this question. Technically, it was none of my business. Iris confirmed this!

"That's none of your business!" she exclaimed.

"Were you following us?" asked Dominic. He sounded hurt. Tara was silent and she wouldn't look me in the eye.

"I did follow you," I said, "from Ghiradelli's. You have to admit this looks rather suspicious. I followed a hunch."

"What's suspicious?" asked Dominic.

"You and Iris friends?" I replied. "The recent thefts. A pawnshop. C'mon."

"Again," said Iris, "it's none of your business, is it? This isn't the first time you've meddled in my affairs, Nora, and I don't like it. As far as I'm concerned, you're finished. Don't come back. I'll notify the school on Monday."

Just then a man came out of the pawnshop. He looked surprised. "Iris, what is this?" he asked.

"One of the student nurses from Marian Manor," said Iris. "She followed us." The man slapped his forehead with the palm of his hand and said, "Iris, I told you this wasn't a good idea. If you weren't my sister ..."

"Shut up, Tommy," said Iris. "I have everything under control."

"Well, I have more bad news for you," I said. "The police are on their way. They should be here any minute."

"Great," said Tommy. He hurried back into the shop.

Iris turned and called after him, "Tommy!" Then, she looked back at me. "You'll pay for this, Nora Brady." She quickly followed her brother into the shop.

"I thought we were friends," said Dominic, shaking his head. He stepped to the doorway of the shop. "Iris" he called. "Tara and I are leaving. Now."

I had nothing to say. Dominic was right. We had been friends. I hadn't had much to go on, except my gut, but my gut had told me there was something wrong. I wanted to melt into the pavement before the police arrived. That wasn't going to happen, however. I had the feeling the police wouldn't find any stolen property. I could see Dominic no longer had the black satchel. This encounter was likely to be an embarrassing waste of time.

A squad car pulled up before anyone had a chance to leave. Two uniformed officers took statements from all of us, but then, just as I had anticipated, they had to let everyone go. It was my word against the word of the other four. The officers couldn't do much in the pawnshop either as search warrants took time.

It was starting to get dark and I had to find my way back to the cable car. I rode down to the waterfront with a heavy heart and retrieved my car. I turned off my cell. I didn't want any more discussion with Dan. The only good part to the day was seeing my friends. They were impressed with my detective work and they laughed when I told them Iris had fired me. "You always were getting into some kind of trouble as a kid," they said. "You'll find a way out." That made me feel better.

On Sunday morning I drove back to Jacobsport. I was so happy to be back in my own apartment. I was tired after the long drive and I didn't want to talk with anyone. I didn't know how much anyone knew, as yet. I thought of the people I should call. I knew I had to call Dan. He picked up on the first ring.

"Please don't say I told you so," I said.

"O.K., but why can't you just let the police do its job?" asked Dan. I didn't reply. "So what happened when the police got there?" he asked.

"They just took our statements," I said.

"I mean, what did Iris say?" asked Dan.

"That she was visiting her brother," I replied.

"And what did she say to you?" he continued.

"Well, I'm fired, if that's what you mean," I said, "and she's threatening to sue me for defamation of character, whatever that means."

"I'm sorry to hear that," said Dan, "but what did you expect? And can she really fire a student?"

"Apparently, she can," I said. "You know, I didn't really think this through. I just knew something had to be done."

"And that was your first mistake," said Dan.

"If I thought about everything that could go wrong, every time I did something, nothing would ever get done," I countered.

"O.K.," said Dan. "I guess you could use a little good news."

"What would that be?" I asked.

"The San Francisco police have been watching Tommy's shop for some time," said Dan, "but it takes time. You gave them more ammunition."

"So what do I do now?" I asked.

"Nothing as far as the police is concerned," said Dan. "It would be really good, however, if you could find a way to get back into Marian Manor. We could use someone on the inside, even if that someone doesn't always play by the rules."

"I could grovel," I said. "If I could talk with Jean or Sam first, they might be able to sway Iris. I do need to say, however, that I'm not very good at groveling."

"Big surprise," said Dan. "Go back to work. Humility is a virtue."

"I'll see what I can do," I said. We said goodbye and Dan promised to touch base sometime in the coming week. After that I called Jean at home and explained the whole situation to her. She was dumbfounded.

"Nora, are you nuts?" she asked.

"I know. I know," I said, "but do you think you could talk with Sam and see if there's any way I could still keep my place. It will throw everything off if I have to start over someplace else."

"I don't know if it'll help, Nora," said Jean, "but I'll see what I can do. I really don't want to lose you."

"Thanks, Jean," I said, hanging up.

It had been a beautiful morning, but now the fog was in and it was perfect for snuggling under an afghan, reading and dozing. About 6:00 Jean called to say that she had talked with Sam. He hadn't reached Iris, so he was uncertain what to do. Sam said he would give me a three-day suspension, which would give him time to sort things out. I could return to work on Thursday, unless I heard otherwise. I thanked Jean profusely and hung up. What was I going to do for three days? And what was I going to do about Dominic, Tara and Iris?? And another thought: was Sam part of all this?

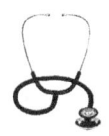

Chapter 16

The next three days passed remarkably fast. I decided to consider the suspension a mini-vacation and I read, watched movies and cleaned my apartment. I visited Stella and I helped Pamela finish up preparing for Stella's homecoming. When I stopped in at Marian Manor, I got by with vague answers to questions as to why I was off.

Even Tina didn't push for an explanation. She seemed to know I was involved in something I couldn't discuss. She had done very well in the marathon, placing second in the women's division. She had a lot to tell me and I hated not telling her the truth about my weekend. It was all very odd. Apparently neither Dominic nor Tara had said anything to anyone about me. It didn't seem fair that I was suspended and they were still working.

I went back to work on Thursday as if nothing had happened. My scrubs were neatly pressed and I had tried a new shampoo that really did seem to make my hair shinier. I felt good. Ready for whatever.

Jean gave me my same assignment, but I was working with one of the aides from 2 East as Dominic was off. Tara was working with Tina and did her best to avoid me, which was fine with me. Jean and I had talked about re-assigning either Dominic or me so we wouldn't have to work together, at least until everything was sorted out. Apparently, Dominic had also talked to Jean, although he didn't give any special reason for his not wanting to work with me.

I was setting up morning meds when Mr. Parker and Mr. Jessel came walking down the hall. Right on time. I reached for the bottle of whiskey I had set on the bottom shelf of my cart and I poured the two shots.

"Good morning, Nora," said Mr. Jessel. "Where have you been? We were beginning to worry. We thought you might've up and quit. Run off to marry one of those many boyfriends!"

"What boyfriends?" I asked, smiling and recapping the whiskey bottle.

"That's for you to tell us," said Mr. Parker. "What about that nice police detective we keep seeing around here? He seems to spend a lot of time talking with you."

"He does not," I laughed, handing them their shot glasses. "Besides, what do I need with him when I have the two of you?"

"Hey, did you hear we might be twins?" asked Mr. Jessel, setting his glass back on the corner of my cart.

"Well Kathy told me there was a possibility," I answered. "She thought maybe there was a test to prove it."

"Yeh, she thinks that the best way would be to get a DNA done," continued Mr. Jessel, "but we're thinking it's not really necessary. We already feel like brothers and, for us, that's all that matters." He smiled and patted Mr. Parker's shoulder. "Imagine, after all these years, I have a brother."

"I pretty much knew from the first time I set eyes on him," said Mr. Parker, setting his glass back on the other side of my cart. "It was like looking in a mirror. I just thought it was all in my head, so I asked Kathy to help me check it out. I didn't know he felt the same way."

"I'm really happy for you two," I said. "Are we going to have some kind of a celebration?"

"We haven't decided yet," said Mr. Jessel.

"Well, there are plenty of us and we all like parties," I said.

As the two men walked on down the hall towards the dining room, I asked myself why I hadn't used the term DNA when I mentioned the testing. Just because someone's elderly doesn't mean he isn't keeping up with what's going on in the world. These two probably knew more about DNA than most of the nursing staff. They were intelligent men who just needed help with some of their physical problems. It was insulting to talk down to them, and I would not to do that again.

It was busy as usual and I kept going until about 10:30 when Jean came to tell me that Sam Clayton wanted to meet with me in his office. For the first time that day, I felt a lead weight sitting in the middle of my stomach. "Suck it up," I said to myself. "You got yourself into this and now it's time to take the consequences." My mother said everything happens for a reason. I wonder what she'd say about this.

When I got downstairs, Helen, Sam's secretary, told me to go ahead into his office. "He's expecting you," she said. I had never been in Sam's office before. Like the conference room, the furniture was polished walnut and the drapes were floral. A small, matching floral sofa was under the window and the same thick carpeting was at my feet. Several large plants were artfully placed around the room and there was a collection of diplomas, certificates and awards on the walls.

Sam was standing over by the window. His shoulders were slumped and he looked tired and somewhat rumpled. He motioned for me to take a seat. "Good morning, Nora," he said, turning from the window. "I'm just waiting for Detective Maguire."

"Oh, he's joining us?" I asked. "Why?"

"You seem to have some very good friends, Nora," said Sam. "First, Jean calls, begging me to keep you on. I didn't even know Iris had suspended you. Or whatever it is we do to students. Then Detective Maguire calls, making the same request. He's the one who wanted this meeting."

Looking at Sam this morning, I now felt certain that whatever Iris was up to, he was not involved. "Have you talked with Mrs. Clayton?" I asked.

"I spoke with her on Sunday and again yesterday, but she didn't tell me much," said Sam. "She said she would be spending more time with her brother. She told me you followed her into the city." He looked over at me with questions in his eyes. "She said your behavior was strange and thoroughly unprofessional."

"Well, technically, I didn't follow her," I said. "But, if you believed her, why did you let me come back?"

"Well, I was convinced by your friends that maybe there was more to the story," said Sam. "It seems, according to Jean, that you accused Iris of being a thief. Is that right?" He looked me squarely in the eye.

"While I never said the words, I did call the police," I explained.

"Why?" asked Sam. I retraced that afternoon in San Francisco and I told him about my call to Dan outside the pawnshop.

"This is so hard to believe," said Sam. "It's true that we've had some minor financial problems, but neither I nor Iris would ever do anything to endanger the safety or well-being of our residents." Just then, there was a knock at the door and Dan entered. Sam took a seat behind his desk. Dan and I sat across from him. "I can't believe that Iris would hurt a fly," said Sam, leaning forward and looking more pathetic as each minute passed.

"I know this is difficult for you, Sam," said Dan. "Aside from the thefts, I just received the results of June Michaels' autopsy. Her death was the direct result of an overdose—one of her heart medicines. Whether this was accidental or intentional, we don't know, but the amount would indicate that it was intentional."

"What does that have to do with Iris?" asked Sam.

"It's a medication your wife also takes," said Dan. "It's a common medicine, so that doesn't mean very much, but it is a factor." Dan paused. "A more important factor is that June Michaels had made Marian Manor the chief beneficiary in her will. Did you know that?"

"No, I didn't know that," said Sam, turning very pale. "Iris handled all the financial paperwork." He leaned back in his chair. He looked pale and beads of perspiration had formed along his hairline and upper lip.

"Sam, are you O.K.?" I asked. "You don't look very good."

"I'm just very tired," said Sam. "And very sad," he added. He was looking down at his hands. The right fingers were playing with the wedding band on his left hand.

"I'm sorry to be the one to tell you this," said Dan. "I wanted Nora down here because she's familiar with these cases and she may be able to help us."

"What can I do?" I asked.

"First off, we need to act as if this past weekend never happened," said Dan. "Apparently that's what our three suspects have done. It appears they haven't told anyone, except you, Sam, about the run in with Nora and the police."

"Then what?" I asked.

"Then, we set up a decoy," said Dan.

"A decoy?" asked Sam, looking up.

"It will be one of our own," said Dan. "A new resident. On 2 West. The new resident will be slightly confused, have plenty of family jewelry and no relatives. He'll be so grateful to Marian Manor for all the good care he's receiving, that he'll want all of his assets to go to Marian Manor in the event of his death. Just like June Michaels and probably like Harriet Allen."

"Harriet Allen?" Sam asked, looking confused. "Are you suggesting that Mrs. Allen was also a victim?"

"I'm not suggesting this," said Dan, "but apparently she has some friends in high places and they seem to have a lot of questions. They've asked us to look into her death."

Sam seemed to shrivel in his chair. "Are you sure you're O.K., Sam?" I asked.

"I'm O.K.," said Sam. "Let's get on with this."

Dan and I looked at each other. "So how will we know if things are missing, if this new resident's confused?" I asked.

"Good question, Nora," said Dan. "O.K. He won't be confused, just forgetful.

Will that work?"

"That should work," I said.

"Any problems with this, Sam?" Dan asked.

"I don't know if I can keep a secret from Iris," said Sam. His voice cracked and he looked close to tears.

"Well it looks like you don't have much day to day contact with the residents," said Dan. "Is that right?"

"That's right," answered Sam. "I make rounds on the units, but Iris does most of the individual work with the residents."

"Then you shouldn't even have to discuss this new resident with Iris," said Dan, "unless she brings him up. Just talk about whatever it is you usually talk about."

"When does the new resident come?" I asked.

"He's already here," said Dan. "It's Isaac Lowenstein."

"Mr. Lowenstein?" Sam and I gasped. "He's really disabled! How can he help with this plan?" I asked.

"He is disabled and he does need your help," said Dan. "He's been living in a nursing home down south, so you've been able to get all his paperwork. But, he's also a retired police detective and the police take the safety of nursing home residents very seriously. When all this started, we began looking for 'a plant,' someone we could have on the inside. We moved him up here under the guise of his having a nephew in Jacobsport. His last surviving relative. We'll arrange for that nephew to be in a fatal crash."

"But Mr. Lowenstein doesn't seem forgetful and I haven't noticed any jewelry," I pointed out. "And please tell me no one really dies."

"No one dies," said Dan, pausing. "Here's the plan. Mr. Lowenstein is going to have a little stroke, from which he will recover, but his memory won't be good. He's going to decide he has some affairs he needs to get in order. He's going to talk with Iris and he'll let her know that he has a safety deposit box he wants to inspect. He'll ask Iris to go with him. The box will contain a number of family heirlooms, including jewelry, coins and certain deeds. He'll explain to Iris that he has no one to leave this to now that his nephew has died."

"I don't know if I can keep up this front with Iris," said Sam.

"In that case, we're recommending you take a vacation," said Dan.

"A vacation?" exclaimed Sam. "Who will run this place?"

"We have someone who's a licensed administrator, someone who goes from home to home, relieving administrators who need to get away," said Dan.

"And what do I tell Iris?" asked Sam.

"The truth," said Dan. "You're completely upset by all the recent events and you need to get away for a few weeks."

"What if she wants to come with me?" asked Sam.

"You tell her you need this time to yourself," said Dan.

"I need to think about this," said Sam. "I need to talk with Iris."

"There isn't time to think," said Dan. "I need to know if you are in or out. We start today. If there's any question of your ability to do this, then you're out of here."

Sam lowered his head onto his tented fingers. No one said anything for several minutes. When Sam raised his head, there was a spark of life in his eyes. "I'm staying," he said. "Marian Manor was dedicated to the memory of my mother. She fought for the rights of the elderly and I can't do any less. Whatever happens, I have to remember this. I brought Iris here, and if she's to go, I'll be the one to see to that."

I wanted to shout "Yeh! Good for you, Sam," but I didn't. Dan extended his hand to Sam and they shook

"There's nothing to do now, but wait for Iris," said Dan.

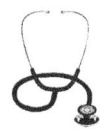

Chapter 17

Friday morning. I didn't sleep well the previous night. I expected to have a big confrontation with Dominic, but as with Tara, he simply avoided me. Jean reassigned Lonnie to work with me and I knew that made for one unhappy aide. "What's with all these changes?" Lonnie asked with a whine.

Jean jumped in explaining that the more variety we had, the more we would learn. And we would be better caregivers because of this. "So why don't you switch the nurses?" asked Lonnie. "They could do other teams."

"One thing at a time," said Jean.

The residents were not happy about the changes either, but they accepted Jean's reasons. One resident who never seemed to question things was Mr. Lowenstein. I began to see him in a different light. He was cheerful, interested in talking to everyone and he participated in all of Kathy's activities. He must have been a different kind of detective from Dan Maguire who didn't talk any more than was absolutely necessary.

I wondered if Dan had spoken with Dr. McCain, Mr. Lowenstein's doctor. If Mr. Lowenstein were going to have a stroke, we would need to send him to the hospital for evaluation. There would be a lot of unnecessary tests charged to insurance. This didn't seem right. Also, if I was the only one aware of this charade, then I should be the one who found Mr. Lowenstein. I should also be the one to report the incident to Dr. McCain and I, as a student, couldn't take any doctor's orders. Unfortunately, I hadn't thought of all this the day before. I hoped Mr. Lowenstein wasn't going to have his stroke before I had a chance to call Dan. I tried to put a call through at lunch, but all I got was voice mail.

"And just what are you doing?" asked Tina, coming up behind me at the phone outside our lounge area. I didn't have my cell with me.

"I'm calling Dan Maguire," I said.

"So, there is something going on between you two, huh?" laughed Tina, "and you haven't even told your best friend."

"It's not what you think," I said. "I keep telling you that." I couldn't tell Tina the real reason for my call and I didn't want her to think I was really interested in Dan, because, of course, I wasn't. On the other hand, he had said we would probably have to make it seem like we were interested in each other in order to maintain our communication. It was hard being part of something I couldn't share with my best friends. I felt dishonest.

"So what is it?" asked Tina.

"Well, I was going to see if he was available to play in that golf tournament next month. You know, the one that's raising money for children's services," I explained lamely. "I already asked Jimmy, but he's going to be out of town. He suggested I try Dan."

"But why Dan?" asked Tina. "And why didn't you ask me?"

"You don't even play golf!" I exclaimed.

"It's a fund raiser," she said. "I don't really have to play. I just have to pay my fee and show up. Hit a little ball with a stick. I can do that."

"So do you want to play?" I asked reluctantly.

"No, I'm busy," said Tina, laughing. "I just wanted to harass you. I hope Dan is free."

I smiled wanly as we started walking back to the unit. My sense of frustration was only compounded when we got back, as there was Iris standing at the desk. "Miss Brady, I want to see you in Jean's office!" she said harshly. I was in for it now and Jean was not around to rescue me.

"I don't know how you had the nerve to come back here," said Iris after closing the door to Jean's office. Neither of us bothered to sit down. We knew this wasn't going to take long. Iris had crossed her arms tightly across her chest. She was braced for battle I tried to stay loose. Iris did unnerve me, but I didn't want her to know this. "Somehow you managed to get to Sam before I did," she continued, "but this is not over. I promise you I will do everything in my power to get you out of here. I already have a call in to your instructor, Mrs. Floyd. You're going to find it very difficult to get another placement."

We stared at each other for a minute or so. Sparks flew from Iris' eyes, while I kept mine neutral. "Are we done?" I asked politely. "I have work to do." She nodded and turned her back. If only I wasn't a student. I had no power. If I were a nurse, she couldn't do much to stop me from getting another job, unless I had done something to violate my nursing license. There are laws to protect people from this kind of employer.

Unfortunately, I was not a nurse. Yet.

When I left the office, everyone was staring at me. Apparently, they had heard Iris. Dominic was wearing a tight smile. Curiosity was evident, but I didn't volunteer any explanation. I couldn't explain anything without spilling the beans about Iris as a suspect in the thefts. I just had to wait.

The afternoon dragged and I was anxious to go home. I wanted to put my feet up, and escape into a good book. I didn't want to think about anyone or anything. Deborah asked if I was free for dinner, but I declined. Tina asked if I was interested in going to a movie, but I said 'no' to that as well.

When I finally did get home, I did exactly what I had been dreaming about all day. I changed into some sweats and put on some Dave Mathews. Then I made some tea, curled up on the couch and opened my new Sue Grafton mystery. I debated about taking the phone off the hook, but I decided to screen calls instead. I had forgotten my call to Dan at lunchtime.

I dozed off while reading and slept through supper. About 8:00 the phone rang. It was Dan returning my call. "I hope this isn't too late," he said. "It's been crazy down here."

"No, it's a good thing you called," I said. "I fell asleep on the couch. It wasn't my best day."

"Why's that?" asked Dan.

"Well, for one thing, I had my first run in with Iris and she's out for blood," I replied.

"Sorry to hear that," he said, "but I'm sure that's not why you called me. I know you can take care of yourself."

"I called because I wondered if you'd talked with Dr. McCain," I said, somewhat irritated that he wasn't more sympathetic to my problem. I explained the problems with Mr. Lowenstein faking a stroke.

"Good points," said Dan. "No, I didn't talk with Dr. McCain, but I'll do so first thing in the morning. Have you thought of a way to call the report to Dr. McCain, so he'll know it's really part of the plan and not a true emergency?"

"I've been thinking," I said. "By the way, to cover my tracks today, I had to tell Tina I was calling you about that fund raising golf tournament next month. I think Jimmy and I mentioned it the other day. Are you free?"

"I'll check my schedule," said Dan.

"It's O.K. if you're not," I said. "I just wanted to be sure I asked you, since I said I was doing that."

"No, I'd like to play again," said Dan. "I really will check my schedule. When do the reservations have to be in?"

"I don't know," I replied, "but I'll check."

"O.K. then. I'll call you tomorrow after I talk with Dr. McCain," said Dan. "We need to get moving on this."

After we said good night, I lay staring up at the ceiling for several minutes, not thinking of anything. Finally, I dragged myself up off the couch and into the kitchen. I thought about fixing something to eat before I went to bed, but I really wasn't hungry. I was just tired, so I went to bed. Six a.m. came way too soon.

Saturday wasn't much better at work. By this time the staff knew something else was going on, other than Jean wanting staff to work with different teams. "What's with you and Dominic?" asked Tina, when we had a minute to ourselves.

"What do you mean?" I asked innocently.

"You know exactly what I mean," said Tina irritably. "Everyone knows that something's going on. It's not just you and Dominic. It's you and Tara too. What's happened?"

I didn't say anything. I just looked at her.

"Does this have anything to do with what's been happening around here?" asked Tina. "I mean these thefts or the deaths of Melba Jones and June Michaels?"

"I really don't want to talk about this," I said. "I just don't trust many people these days."

"Does that include me?" asked Tina huffily.

"Of course not," I said.

"Well you guys better get it sorted out," said Tina, "because it's affecting everyone up here. It's a small staff and we have to work together."

"It will be sorted out, I promise," I said. Tina gave me a reluctant smile and went off to work at her med cart.

I was working at my med cart when I saw Dr. McCain coming down the hall. He came over to me, glancing around to be sure there was no one who would overhear us. "I spoke with Detective Maguire this morning," he said. "I know what you two are trying to do, but I have some reservations."

"What concerns you?" I asked.

"You do know Mr. Lowenstein's health is not the best, don't you?" he asked.

"I know," I answered, "but apparently he volunteered to help with this."

"Still, I want to be sure it's you I talk with if something happens," he said.

"If it's not me, then you'll have to believe the situation is real," I said. "I've been thinking about this a lot. If it's fake, then I'll tell you I think Mr. Lowenstein is going to be fine, that he doesn't need to go to the hospital. You can tell me you'll be coming in to see him later and that's what I'll tell the staff."

"That sounds pretty good," said Dr. McCain. "This 'cloak and dagger' stuff is not my thing, but I do want to help."

"Are you going to be around the next few days?" I asked.

"I have no plans to go away," said Dr. McCain. "Why do you ask?"

"I just want to be sure if I call you, that I get you and not another doctor who may be taking call," I explained. Doctors relieve each other for days off, or weekends and holidays.

"Good point," he said. "Now I guess I should have a little talk with Mr. Lowenstein and see what his plan is. I'll let you know." Dr. McCain walked off down the hall to find Mr. Lowenstein. He returned a short time later and told me they had decided to launch the plan the next morning. The sooner the better.

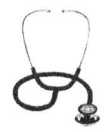

Chapter 18

Sunday morning I awoke with a sense of excitement. I just knew that soon we would be able to prove who was at the bottom of these thefts and who had murdered June Michaels. I was less optimistic about recovering the missing jewelry, however, and my enthusiasm received a splash of cold water when I went out to the garage. I wasn't going to make it to Marian Manor for a while, as I discovered a flat tire. I couldn't believe this had happened to me today, of all days. Fortunately, the auto club was able to send someone out to fix the tire within thirty minutes. I caught the mechanic just before he went to church.

By the time I got to work, everyone else was well into the morning routine. I hated being late for work. I always felt disorganized. Even though I wasn't that late, I felt rushed. Again, I asked myself "why today of all days?"

Tina filled me in on my assignment and there was nothing new on my team. I passed the morning meds and did my morning treatments. Then I went to visit with Charlotte Danner who, it was reported, wasn't very happy. Actually, Mrs. Danner was often rather unhappy and had been even more so since the death of June Michaels. The staff continually tried to get her involved in activities, but she just wasn't interested. We thought an interest in something outside of herself, helping someone else, might make her feel better. Even her family, who lived nearby, seemed to avoid visiting her. If the family did come to visit, they never stayed for long.

When Mrs. Danner was having a particularly bad day, she would snap at everyone—everyone except me as I had "saved her life." Today was one of those days. I sat on the side of her bed while she sat in her chair by the window. She gave me her list of complaints and I tried to smooth things over. She wasn't listening to me and I was trying not to appear too frustrated. Suddenly I heard a commotion in the hall and someone was yelling my name. I bolted from the bed and flew out into the hall. I had, momentarily, completely forgotten about Isaac Lowenstein and our plan.

"Nora! It's Mr. Lowenstein! I think he's having a stroke!" exclaimed Lonnie. She was standing in the doorway of Mr. Lowenstein's room. I slipped around her and went to kneel beside Mr. Lowenstein who was lying on his bed. His eyes were closed and his mouth appeared to be drooping on the left side.

"What's the problem in here?" said another female voice from the hall. It was Dr. Graves.

"I think Mr. Lowenstein is having a stroke," explained Lonnie.

As I bent over Mr. Lowenstein, I called his name and gently shook him. He opened his eyes briefly and winked at me. I called for our blood pressure monitor and started listening to his chest. Then, Dr. Graves joined us at the bedside, asking what had happened. I gave her a brief rundown and then wondered what this was going to do to our plan. What was Dr. Graves doing here on a Sunday?

"I think you'd better go ahead and call for an ambulance," said Dr. Graves.

"I think I'll try to reach Dr. McCain first," I said, walking towards the door, pausing only for a second at the doorway to look back at Mr. Lowenstein. It looked like he was waking up, but he was having some difficulty saying his words.

"I said 'call an ambulance,'" Dr. Graves repeated. She was checking Mr. Lowenstein's ability to move his arms and his legs. She didn't look up at me. I ran for the phone, praying furiously that Dr. McCain's answering service would let me speak with him immediately. In moments he was on the phone, and, as we had planned, I told him we thought Mr. Lowenstein was having a stroke. I told Dr. McCain that Mr. Lowenstein seemed to be doing better and I didn't think he needed to go to the hospital. Dr. McCain was confirming he would be coming in when the phone was ripped out of my hand.

"Joe, this is Sara Graves. I think this patient of yours should be seen in the ER," said Dr. Graves. "You know the three hour protocol for suspected strokes." She appeared to be listening to whatever Dr. McCain was saying, while the frown lines deepened in her brow. "O.K., Joe. But she's only a student. O.K. It's your patient. I was just trying to help." She hung up the phone and turned to me.

"I don't know what's going on here, Nora, but something's fishy," said Dr. Graves. "This patient belongs in the ER. I don't know why Joe McCain is ignoring protocol, but I think you're responsible for this somehow. I don't know what you said to him, but I'll find out."

"I just thought Dr. McCain would be more familiar with this man's history, Dr. Graves," I started to explain.

"But you ignored my order to call the ambulance," said Dr. Graves. "I find that very disturbing. If anything happens to this patient, it will be on your head." She then asked Tina for Mr. Lowenstein's chart, so that she might make a note. While her back was turned to me, I picked up Mr. Lowenstein's chart, which was at the bottom of my stack of charts and I slipped it into the bottom drawer of the desk. I didn't want her making a note about an incident that wasn't real. When she and Tina couldn't find the chart, even after looking through mine, she requested a blank progress note, made her note and handed it to me.

"This had better make it into Mr. Lowenstein's chart," said Dr. Graves, as she walked off the unit. I took the note, folded it and placed it on my clipboard to give to Dan.

I went back into Mr. Lowenstein's room. Lonnie was checking his blood pressure again. "His blood pressure is fine," said Lonnie. "I don't get it. Shouldn't his blood pressure be up?"

"It depends," I said. "It could have been up for a short while and then gone back down again. You would expect it to stay up, but not always." I leaned over to check Mr. Lowenstein, hoping my explanation would satisfy Lonnie. "How are you doing?" I asked.

"Better," he replied.

"Do you remember what happened?" I continued. Lonnie was watching us closely. I could see she was really concerned, that she cared about Mr. Lowenstein. I was a little surprised.

"No. The last thing I remember is getting a phone call from my nephew's girlfriend," he said slowly. "She said Tim, my nephew, was on his way to Garberville when his cycle went off the side of the road. She told me he was killed instantly." Tears started to well up in Mr. Lowenstein's eyes. I was impressed that he could play this part so well.

"Someone just told you that on the phone?" I asked. "I can't believe it! They should have waited until you had someone with you." Lonnie was nodding agreement. Maybe Lonnie and I were more alike than I thought. I'd have to consider this later.

"She was afraid I'd hear it on the TV," he explained. "There aren't any other relatives. She really didn't have any choice."

After Lonnie left the room, I told Mr. Lowenstein what a great performance I thought he had given. I asked him how he could cry like that.

"It actually happened to me," he said. "I don't have to fake these tears. I feel them every time I think of my nephew. He was a great kid. More like my son." Mr. Lowenstein paused and looked away. "I miss him. Dan Maguire reminds me a lot of my nephew, Tim. He was also a detective."

"Well, I think it's wonderful what you're doing, helping us out," I said. "I, for one, really appreciate it."

"I'm just glad to be of service," he said. "It was hard for me to retire. It's nice to be of use again."

"Well, now I guess we just wait a few days," I said, "and then you ask to talk with Iris. Is that right?"

"That's the plan," he replied. "I guess I need to start forgetting things too. Any ideas?"

"Well, you could forget which drawer you put things in," I replied. "You could forget which room is yours. You could forget our names."

"Well, some of that won't be hard to do," he laughed, "especially the names."

"Join the club!" I said. We both laughed and then I remembered that anyone could be out in the hall and we had better not be too loud.

Later that afternoon, Dr. McCain did come in. He checked Mr. Lowenstein's memory, his ability to move his arms and legs, his ability to feel things and his speech. He wrote a note in the chart, but he didn't say a word about a stroke. I asked him about my run in with Dr. Graves, but he told me not to worry. Everything would be out in the open eventually and Dr. Graves would understand what we were doing. I hoped so. I didn't want anyone criticizing Dr. McCain.

Before I left work that afternoon, I stopped in to spend some time with Stella. While we saw each other every day now, there wasn't a lot of time to visit. Pamela was in Stella's room, but she was getting ready to leave. She'd brought Eugene in to visit Stella and was putting him back into his carrier for the trip home. They were discussing the plans for Stella to go home in the coming week.

Stella was looking forward to this. She'd been at Marian Manor for almost two weeks and had been gone from her own home for nearly three. She missed Eugene and she missed her independence. Pamela had arranged for someone to come in and help Stella on a daily basis and the home health nurse would also be checking on Stella's progress. In addition, Stella would have home physical therapy and occupational therapy for several weeks, just to be sure that she was managing safely. While Stella wasn't very excited about having all these new people in her home, she was so anxious to go home she was willing to accept any conditions. I was also looking forward to having Stella home again. She was like family to me and I missed having her downstairs.

"What's the first thing that you're going to do when you go home, Stella?" I asked.

"Take a long, hot bath," she replied.

"Now, Mom, you know you can't get into the tub just yet," said Pamela. "You need to get a little more flexibility in those legs of yours. You can take a long, hot shower though. We have it all set up. Nora helped."

"Pamela had Charles add grab bars for you to hold onto in the shower," I said, "and now there's a seat for you to rest on as well. She also put in a new shower hose, so you can control where the water goes, like we have here."

"I don't want my bathroom looking like I'm in a hospital," said Stella.

"You won't even see any of this stuff until you get in the shower," I said, "and it'll make it easier for you to do things for yourself."

"Well I'm so happy to get home, I really don't care what you've done, dear," said Stella, looking over towards Pamela.

"You'll love it," I said. "I'm on my way home now and I'm off tomorrow, so I'll see you on Tuesday." I leaned over to give Stella a kiss on the cheek.

"Oh Nora, could you do me a favor and take Eugene back with you, as long as you're going home?" asked Pamela.

"Sure, no problem," I said, taking the carrier from Pamela's outstretched arm. They both thanked me. Eugene was hissing and meowing in the carrier, which said he didn't much like the carrier and he wanted everyone to know this. We said good-bye and left Stella to get ready for dinner.

When I got home that evening, there was a message from Dan on the answering machine. He said he'd heard all had gone well. No need to call him back. Everyone knew I was off the next day, so part two of our plan would go into effect on Tuesday. Isaac Lowenstein would approach Iris about going to his safety deposit box. Then he would request information on how to go about changing his will.

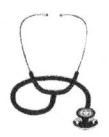

Chapter 19

When I returned to work on Tuesday, the nurses reported that Mr. Lowenstein was doing much better. He didn't seem to have any weakness in his arms or legs and his speech was fine. He was up with his friends Herman Jessel and John Parker. The only question anyone seemed to have concerned how Dr. McCain had handled the situation.

"I always thought Dr. McCain was a good doctor," said Tina. "I can't believe he didn't send Mr. Lowenstein to the ER, at least for an evaluation and a CT scan."

"But he knew Mr. Lowenstein's history," I argued, "and he knew these episodes were not that unusual for Mr. Lowenstein." I wanted to defend Dr. McCain's reputation. Hopefully, everything would soon be clear. I was guessing that Dr. Graves had not helped the situation.

"Still, it just seems odd to me," said Tina. Then she changed the subject. "By the way, Kathy was up here yesterday and she wants to plan something special for Herman Jessel and John Parker—something to celebrate their being brothers."

"That's wonderful," I said. "Did they have the DNA done?"

"The DNA was done," said Tina, "but our guys don't want to know the results."

"Good for them," I said.

"Isn't that something?" said Tina. "Imagine finding your brother after all these years."

"It sure is," I said. "What are the chances?"

As we were sitting at the nurses' station, planning our day's work, Mr. Lowenstein stopped at the desk on his way to breakfast. "Nora, would you please tell Jean I'd like to speak with her when she has a minute?"

"Sure," I said. "Can I tell her what it's about?"

"Oh, I just want to see about straightening out some legal matters," he replied.

"Sure, Mr. Lowenstein," I said. "She's at a meeting now, but I'll tell her as soon as she gets back. She'll probably have to arrange a meeting for you with Mrs. Clayton. She's the one who handles all those matters."

"Well, maybe I'll just walk down to Mrs. Clayton's office," he said. "I can use the exercise."

"Good for you," I said. "Hey, where are your buddies?"

"They're on their way," he said, pointing down the hallway. As Herman Jessel and John Parker got closer, he added: "You know they're a lot older than me."

"Who are you talking about, old man," asked John Parker. "You know that age is a state of mind and I could whip your skinny butt anytime, anywhere." The three of them were shaking their fists at one another, but they were laughing.

"O.K. you guys," I said. "No fighting or I'll have to send you to your rooms without breakfast."

"Maybe that's not such a bad thing," said Herman Jessel, grimacing.

"It also means no whiskey," I said.

"You wouldn't," said John Parker.

"Oh yes I would," I laughed.

"And she means it," said Isaac Lowenstein.

"O.K., O.K.," they said in unison. "Whatever you say!"

I finished putting together my care plans and got up to prepare my med cart. The morning went quickly. Mr. Lowenstein found me about 11:00 and said he'd been down to see Iris and they had an appointment after lunch. He was hoping she might also take him to the bank. I secretly hoped all this activity wasn't going to prove to be too much for him.

At 1:30 Jean got a call from Iris, who said she was going to take Mr. Lowenstein to the bank. If they had time, they would also see an attorney. I hoped I would still be on duty when they got back, or I would have to dream up some excuse for staying on the unit. I wanted to talk with Mr. Lowenstein to see how things had gone with Iris.

At 2:00 we got a call from one of our afternoon nurses who was going to be late because she was having some urgent car repairs done. I volunteered to stay over until she arrived. I was relieved that I wouldn't have to invent an excuse.

By 4:00 I was beginning to wonder what had happened with Iris and Mr. Lowenstein and if our plan was really so great. By 5:30 I was still waiting and wondering if I should have called Dan earlier. What if something had happened to Mr. Lowenstein? After all, we might be dealing with a murderer.

When Dawn, the evening nurse, arrived, she was full of apologies. While I couldn't tell her that she had done me a big favor, I did tell her I understood her problem. I had had car problems myself this past week.

While I was in the middle of giving report to Dawn, Mr. Lowenstein arrived back on the unit. He was by himself and he looked very tired. I said hello and finished my report before going in to see him. He was stretched out on his bed when I entered the room. "You look exhausted," I said. "How did things go?"

"I am exhausted. That woman is exhausting," he said. "She talks on, and on, and on. I thought seriously about strangling her.

I do think she took the bait though. Her eyes tripled in size when I opened that safety deposit box. I knew she couldn't wait to get her hands on the jewelry. And she couldn't get me over to the attorney fast enough."

"How did that go?" I asked. "What did he have to say?"

"Well, I brought him my old will, which isn't really my will, and I told him the changes I wanted to make," said Mr. Lowenstein. "He said it would take a few days and he would call when the new will was ready for my signature. The attorney is a real sleazball. I think Dan should look into that guy's affairs too."

"How was Iris during all this?" I asked.

"She couldn't do enough for me," he answered. "'Are you warm enough, Mr. Lowenstein?' 'Do you need anything to drink, Mr. Lowenstein?' 'Can I bring that chair closer to the desk for you, Mr. Lowenstein?' It was nauseating." He mimicked Iris with a high pitched, wheedling voice.

I laughed. "You deserve some kind of medal for all this, Mr. Lowenstein," I crooned, imitating his mimicking of Iris.

He laughed. "There's nothing to do until that new will is signed," he said. "Iris isn't going to pull anything until she's sure that Marian Manor is the beneficiary when I die."

"So how are we going to protect you?" I asked. "We don't know how soon she will act, after the will is signed."

"We'll have to take it day by day," said Mr. Lowenstein. "She's not a very bright woman, so I don't think she's going to be too creative if she tries to kill me,"

"Just the thought of that chills me to the bone," I said. "I wish we had a better idea of how she might have gotten to June Michaels."

"You had better not be trying to weasel your way into the affections of our favorite nurse," came a voice from the hall. It was Herman Jessel and the other "amigo," John Parker. "Why have you kept her here so late?"

"We're having a private discussion," said Mr. Lowenstein. "The girl recognizes quality when she sees it. We didn't want to tell anyone, but we're planning to run away next weekend. Well, she'll be running and I'll be trying to catch up." We laughed.

"This is one situation where the 'best man' did not win," said John Parker to Herman Jessel. "I'll never understand women."

"You three are too much," I said. "You know I love you all and I would never be able to pick just one."

"So run away with all three of us," said Mr. Lowenstein. "I'm willing to share."

"I'm going home," I said. "You three are going to dinner." There was the fragrance of roast beef and gravy in the air. I thought of mashed potatoes and peas. I was hungry!

"You're no fun," they chorused, as I started helping Mr. Lowenstein to his feet.

"I'll see you all tomorrow," I said. "Have a great evening."

As soon as I got home, I called Dan and gave him my report. I expressed my concern about what tricks Iris might pull and questioned how we were going to protect Mr. Lowenstein.

"Isaac is right," said Dan. "Iris isn't going to do anything until the new will is signed and that won't happen for several days. And you're also right in saying we don't know how soon Iris is going to act. We probably need to do some brain-storming about the possibilities of what she'll do and how best to see that she doesn't succeed."

"When do you want to do this?" I asked.

"The sooner, the better," said Dan. "What about this evening?"

"I guess that's O.K.," I said. "I haven't eaten yet. Could we meet somewhere to get a burger or something?" I was still thinking "beef."

"Sure," said Dan. "How about Louie's? I'm going to see if my partner Cait is available. I know she has some thoughts on this case."

"I didn't know you had a partner," I said.

"Well this case didn't seem to warrant two people, so I started alone," he said. "We've added other people along the way, but Cait has been working on it all along."

"O.K., then," I said. "Is it Caitlyn Cruise? I think I remember her from one of the staff meetings."

"That's her," said Dan. "Is 7:30 O.K.? That will give me time to get in touch with Cait."

"That's fine," I said. "See you later." I hung up and found that I was feeling just a little annoyed, but I wasn't sure why. I guess I was feeling a little possessive about the case and I wasn't sure if I wanted to share it with anyone else. I knew this was foolish. We were dealing with life and death and we needed all the help we could get. Besides, it wasn't really "my" case. And, I certainly didn't know anything about police work!

I was early in getting to Louie's, a small restaurant on the coast, just south of Jacobsport. By now I was starving. I hoped Dan and Cait would be on time. They were.

Laughing heartily as they came through the door, they took seats across from me and had to catch their breaths before they could talk.

"What's so funny?" I asked.

"Cait was just telling me about her run-in with our captain today," said Dan. "I guess we shouldn't be disrespectful, but you would have to know this guy."

Dan quickly made the introductions and Cait extended her hand. She had a firm handshake and looked me straight in the eye. I liked her immediately.

"I'm always having run-ins with the captain," said Cait. "I never know when to keep my mouth shut. My husband tells me that all the time."

Cait did not look like she would cause anyone any problems. She was about 5 feet 5, with a good figure and great, sun-bleached, medium length blond hair—the California girl. She was not at all like I pictured any real police detective.

"I'm sorry, but you don't look like a troublemaker," I said.

"Don't let those great looks fool you, Nora," said Dan. "Cait's a black belt and can take on anything."

"Well, if she can take on Iris, then we're in business," I said.

We talked for several hours over our hamburgers, onion rings and multiple cups of coffee. Louie's has great food. Dan had filled Cait in on the basics, but she was interested in hearing more about the staff. Her questions were good, as were her comments. "We really need to keep track of that brother Tommy," she said.

"I'm doing that," said Dan. "I'm checking with SFPD daily."

"Well, I think you've covered all the bases," said Cait. "I'll just continue with our day to day, Dan. You guys can let me know if you need me."

"And you'll let us know when the will is ready for signing, right, Nora?" asked Dan.

"Sure," I replied. "As soon as I know, you'll know."

"I don't think we can do any more or plan anything until Iris makes her move," said Cait. "Nice meeting you, Nora." She extended her hand.

"Nice meeting you, Cait," I said, extending mine.

We all said goodnight. I felt better knowing we were on the same wave length. I knew there wasn't much to do until that will was signed, but I was worried about what would happen after that. My gut was talking to me again. It seemed to be saying that Iris wasn't as stupid as everyone seemed to think. She might pull something unexpected and we might be too late to save Isaac Lowenstein.

Chapter 20

As predicted, the new will was ready for Isaac Lowenstein to sign just two days after that first meeting. Jean suggested that Iris have the attorney bring the will to Marian Manor and save Mr. Lowenstein the trip, but Iris was insistent. The attorney was very busy and she and Mr. Lowenstein must go to his office. Iris scheduled the meeting for the next morning.

"Something doesn't feel right," I told Mr. Lowenstein.

"Nothing about Iris is quite right," he replied. "We just have to go along with her for the moment."

I wanted to talk with Dan. I tried to put a call through to him at lunchtime, but I only got his voice mail again. As I was preparing for afternoon meds, Jean came by. "You're wanted down in Sam Clayton's office again," she said. There were questions in her eyes, but she didn't ask them and I was grateful.

I locked up my cart and walked down to Tina's end of the hall. " I have to run down to Sam's office for a minute," I said. "Will you keep an eye on my team, please? Thanks." I didn't wait for Tina's reply.

Helen, Sam's secretary, was not at her desk when I got there. I knocked and walked in. Sam was sitting at his desk, white-faced and grim. Seated with him were Dan and Cait. "Take a seat," said Dan. "We've had some news."

"Oh?" I said, taking one of the armchairs off to the side. I pulled it closer.

"The detectives in San Francisco finally caught Iris' brother Tommy with the goods," said Dan. He looked at Sam. "In the process of questioning Tommy, it seems he was willing to bargain."

"I can't listen to any more of this," said Sam, jumping out of his chair. "I need to call my attorney."

"I hope it isn't the same one Iris used for Mr. Lowenstein," said Dan. "My partner here has been doing a little checking on him too and we have a number of questions."

"No, Iris and I have different views on attorneys," said Sam.

"Well, you're certainly free to call an attorney, Mr. Clayton," said Cait, "but we don't think you're involved in any wrongdoing."

"I would just feel more comfortable," said Sam. He got up and walked into the outer office. We could hear him talking to someone on the phone. Then he came back in and sat down. "He says I shouldn't talk with you without him, but he can't come right now." Sam paused. He was gripping the edge of the desk. "I don't know what to do," he said. "I know you have to move on this." He looked around at our faces, apparently hoping someone could help him. No one spoke. "O.K.," he said. "Go ahead."

"Anyway," Dan continued, "what Tommy had to say to them was very disturbing. It seems Iris arranged for Tommy to come up here. She and Tommy planned to stage a little hit and run."

"You mean they were going to kill Mr. Lowenstein?" I asked in disbelief. "Run him over?"

"That was the plan," said Dan. "They figured no one would think it was anything other than an accident."

"This is my wife you're talking about," said Sam. "She's not perfect, but I just can't believe she could kill someone."

Dan glanced at Sam, but continued relating the news from

San Francisco. "Iris and Tommy were to time themselves. Just as Iris and Isaac were leaving the attorney's office, Iris would let Isaac start across the street, but she would think of some reason to run back into the attorney's office. Tommy would suddenly pull out from a nearby alley, speed up, hit Isaac and take off. He would be in San Francisco by evening, lost in the crowd.

"In that attorney's neighborhood, there aren't many people walking around. The whole thing would happen so fast, it's unlikely any witness could positively identify either him or the car. Iris and the attorney would claim to be so distraught they would neglect to call '911' immediately. Isaac would be dead before help came. All in all it's not a bad plan, so far as murder goes."

"Does Iris know Tommy was picked up?" I asked.

"No, she doesn't," said Dan, "and we're going to keep it that way."

"What do you mean?" asked Sam.

"We're going to let Iris' plan go as scheduled," said Dan, "only instead of Tommy driving the car, we'll have one of our own men. He'll only appear to hit Isaac and this is where you come in, Nora. We have to make it look like Isaac was hit. You'll need to talk with him and explain what's going on. If Cait or I do this, it's certain to look suspicious and we can't take any chances. We have to catch Iris in the act.

"We'll find out exactly when Iris is taking Isaac to the attorney's. Then we'll have you tape packets of fake blood to Isaac's body, under his clothes, where it's most likely he would suffer injury, if he actually were hit. No one will be looking that closely. Isaac has been through plans like this before, so he knows how to fall. We know it gets harder the older you are, but he assured us he will do whatever needs to be done." Dan and Cait exchanged a look. I guessed they were still a little worried about Mr. Lowenstein.

"Iris told Jean she would take Mr. Lowenstein to the attorney about 9:00 tomorrow morning," I said. "Jean tried to have the attorney come to Marian Manor, but Iris said it wasn't possible." We all looked at each other. "So what happens after the hit?" I asked.

"We'll have some of our own plain clothes people at the scene," said Dan. "They will place the '911' call and it'll be our own ambulance that takes Isaac to a specially prepared room at Harrison Hospital. The room will have multiple cameras and a two-way mirror in place. We expect Iris to pay Isaac a visit to finish the job and we'll be there."

"When do you suppose that will happen?" I asked.

"Not long after Isaac is admitted to the hospital, is my guess," said Dan.

"And Iris doesn't have to talk with Tommy before this?" I asked.

"No, they didn't want any phone calls that could connect them," said Cait.

"How will I get the blood?" I asked.

"I'll drop it off at your place tonight," said Dan.

"How will I get it in here?" I asked. "You know we all carry these see-through bags now."

"That's up to you," said Dan. "We don't have all the answers." He laughed.

"O.K., let's go for it," I said. "I'll talk with Mr. Lowenstein this afternoon."

While the meeting in Sam's office hadn't taken very long, I felt like I was in a different world when I got back to the unit. Everything about this was foreign. Everything a nurse does is geared towards making people feel better and here I was plotting to catch a thief and a murderer by staging an accident. I knew it was for the good of the other residents, but it felt very strange.

When I explained the plan to Mr. Lowenstein, he made few comments. "I've taken a lot of falls," he said. "I know how to do it and no one is going to be watching my performance that closely." He paused and his eyes were trying to reassure me. "I've also worked with fake blood before, so I know exactly where we should place the packets. Ask Dan for some blood capsules for my mouth. A bleeding mouth is a good sign someone is badly hurt and possibly dying."

"That was what we were going for," I said.

"I guess Iris is a little more creative than I gave her credit for," he said.

"That's just what I was thinking," I said. "And I have to say, I can't believe how calm you are about all this. I'm really impressed."

"It's my job, Nora," he said. "Or, it was my job. I'm glad to help."

"O.K.," I said. "I'll plan on coming in a little early tomorrow. You think up some excuse as to why I'm here."

He laughed. "I'll think of something that requires your specific attention!"

When our shift was finished, I was collecting my things and getting ready to leave. "Any plans for the evening?" asked Deborah.

"Not really," I said. "What are you up to?"

"Well, I was going to try that new Thai restaurant down on 4th Street," she replied. "I thought maybe you could join me, if you don't already have plans."

"I'm waiting for a call tonight," I said, "but if we could go early, that would be great."

"How about 5:00?" asked Deborah. "We really haven't had much chance to talk lately and I miss that. I enjoyed our talks when you were staying with me."

"I enjoyed our talks too," I said. "Five o'clock is fine and tonight is really pretty good, because tomorrow Stella is coming home. I'd like to be there for that."

"O.K.," said Deborah. "I'm going home to change and I'll meet you at the restaurant."

"See you later," I called as she walked out the door.

As I was standing at the desk, Jean came by on her way out.

"Everything going O.K.?" she asked. "I know something's going on and that it has to do with these thefts. Just be careful, will you?"

"Of course," I assured her. She gave me a long look, patted my arm and walked away. I picked up my things and waved a goodby to Mr. Lowenstein, who had since been joined by Mr. Jessel and Mr. Parker. I walked down the hall to say good night to Stella. I wished her a good night's sleep, but I knew it would be difficult since she was so excited about going home. Tomorrow would be an exciting day in more ways than one.

When I got home from work, I gave Dan a call to let him know I was going to be out for a while. I also needed to tell him Mr. Lowenstein wanted the blood capsules. I was surprised when Dan answered the phone himself on the first ring.

"I'm glad you called, Nora," he said. "I was just getting ready to call you. I was going to see if you wanted to double check tomorrow's plan over dinner, but I guess you already have plans. I can drop the supplies for Isaac off whenever it's convenient. The blood capsules are a good idea."

"Thanks Dan," I said. "I should be home by 7:00. The blood capsules *are* a good idea, aren't they?"

"That Isaac is a pro," said Dan. "I'll plan on being by about 7:30. See you then."

"O.K., and thanks," I said, hanging up the phone.

Deborah and I had a good dinner and I enjoyed talking with her. There's never enough time to get to know people at work. The more I talked with Deborah, the better I liked her. I wondered how I could have had such a wrong impression. Over dinner I decided to clear the air about some of my suspicions.

"You know, Deborah, I'm ashamed to say this now, but I even suspected you a little," I said. She didn't know the thieves had been identified.

"Me?" said Deborah, with a bewildered look on her face.

"Well, you probably don't remember, but there was one afternoon when I saw you going through June Michaels bedside table," I started to explain. "I saw you put something in your pocket that day. You said you were concerned about ants, but just after that, the necklace and letter opener were gone."

"I remember that," said Deborah, smiling. "I guess it would have looked pretty suspicious. I probably put sugar packets or crackers in my pocket." She paused as if trying to remember. "I never thought of you as the thief, but I did wonder if it was you who leaked everything to the newspaper?"

"Me?" I exclaimed. "Why would you think that?"

"Well, you were the person who seemed the most upset," said Deborah. "Maybe you thought public attention would flush out the thief."

"It wasn't me," I said. "I have no idea who did that. It could even have been someone on one of the other units. Anyway, I'm really glad we've gotten to know each other better."

"Me too," said Deborah. "It's been a rough couple of months for me and I know my mind hasn't been on my work. I really blew that first round with Dr. McCain."

"What do you mean?" I asked innocently. We had never talked about this.

"Well, I should have brushed up on what was new with my team and I didn't," said Deborah. "There's been so much going on with my sisters. I'm afraid when I'm at work, I only do what I absolutely have to do, much of the time."

"Dr. McCain is really fair," I said. "He'll give you another chance. And, I'm sure Jean defended you. She's really good about that."

"I hope so," said Deborah. "I really do like my job and I would miss everyone if I had to leave."

I admired Deborah's devotion to her sisters. I had also come to realize she was a good nurse. She liked working with the residents and it showed. "We should do this more often," I said.

"I agree," said Deborah. "Maybe next time we can include some of the others, like Tina and Dominic. Maybe even Jean."

I didn't tell her about my problem with Dominic and she didn't ask. Thinking of Dominic reminded me I had to get home. Deborah and I parted, promising to organize a staff night out.

Dan dropped by right on time and he had all the supplies with him. "These are really simple to use," he said, picking up one of the fake blood packets. "You can either strap them on or tape them in place."

"I can't believe how small they are," I said, picking up one of the packets. "I should know this, though. It always looks like there's more blood on something than there really is. Our instructors used to make us test this by filling syringes with colored water and squirting them on old sheets." I figured I could probably fit everything into my scrub pockets. My student scrubs did have lots of pockets.

"Would you like some coffee?" I asked.

"I'll take a rain check," Dan replied. "I have another stop to make." I wondered briefly, if that were true or just an excuse.

After Dan left, I went to bed, watched some TV and read for a while. When I finally turned off the light, I was certain I wouldn't sleep a wink, but within minutes I was asleep. I slept right through until morning.

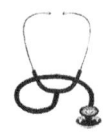

Chapter 21

I bounced out of bed the next morning, took a quick shower, gulped a breakfast shake and got to work about 30 minutes early. This was just the right amount of time to get Mr. Lowenstein taped up and dressed. We didn't want anyone else helping him.

"Someone is going to owe me a new suit after today, you know," he laughed as I was lacing up his good wingtips.

"Mr. Lowenstein!" I exclaimed. "If you help them solve this case, I'm sure Dan will give you just about anything you ask for!"

After we finished, I walked out to the nurses' station just as Jean was coming on the unit. "Nora, what are you doing here so early?" she asked.

"I promised Mr. Lowenstein I would come a little early and help him get dressed for his morning out with Iris," I explained. "She told him they would go for an early lunch after the trip to the attorney's office. He wanted to look his best."

"That was good of you," said Jean with a puzzled look on her face. She didn't, however, say anything else.

As I went ahead with my morning routine, Mr. Lowenstein came down the hall, closely followed by Mr. Jessel and Mr. Parker. "Would you please tell these two to leave me alone," he asked.

"We just want to know who died," said Mr. Jessel.

"He could be going to a wedding, Herman," said Mr. Parker.

This teasing went on until Iris rescued him shortly after breakfast. I guess we couldn't call this a rescue, though, knowing what Iris was planning. The two left arm in arm. I felt nauseous. I felt nauseous all morning. About 10:00 Jean called the nursing staff together. "I have some bad news," she said. "Mr. Lowenstein's been hit by a car. He appears to be in serious condition and has been taken to Harrison Hospital."

"How did it happen?" asked Tina.

"I don't have any details as yet," said Jean, "but I'll keep you posted."

"What should we tell the other residents?" asked Lonnie.

"That we will keep them updated as soon as we hear anything," said Jean. "We don't want to upset anyone more than we have to."

We nodded in agreement and slowly separated, going back to what we had been doing. I didn't know whether to believe the story myself. After all, Mr. Lowenstein could have been injured. I felt bad for the staff and residents. Some people were crying. They didn't know, of course, that this was all staged. I wondered what they would think when Mr. Lowenstein came back in good condition, *if* he came back in good condition. What if Iris had another trick up her sleeve? What if Dan's driver miscalculated and actually hit Mr. Lowenstein? It was hard to wait.

After lunch, Jean tried to call the hospital to check on Mr. Lowenstein's condition. "They can't release any information," she said. "It's a patient privacy thing and as a hit and run, it's now a police case."

"Maybe you could get some information through Detective Maguire," I suggested.

"Good idea, Nora," she replied, picking up the phone again. Dan wasn't there, but she left a message. He called back before the end of our shift. We were gathered around Jean with everyone trying to listen at the same time.

"Mr. Lowenstein is stable," Dan reported, "but he's sedated on a ventilator." A ventilator is a machine that breathes for the patient.

"What about visitors?" asked Jean.

"No visitors," said Dan. "I'll call if anything changes. Maybe you can get more information from Dr. McCain."

"Thanks," said Jean. "I'll try that."

I wanted to see how Mr. Jessel and Mr. Parker were doing. I found them in their room. They never stayed in their room. "Learn anything?" asked Mr. Parker, looking up as I entered. He was reading the paper. Mr. Jessel was playing solitaire. Neither smiled.

"He's holding his own," I said, explaining the ventilator. "What about you two?"

"We're fine," said Mr. Jessel. "Just keep us posted, O.K.?" He was gruff.

"Try not to worry," I said. "We'll let you know whatever we learn." I felt guilty about the pain they were feeling for their friend.

Mr. Lowenstein's accident put something of a damper on Stella's farewell. Pamela came to pick her up and I promised to have dinner with them that evening. Then we would celebrate.

Part of me couldn't wait to get home, so I could talk with Dan and find out what had happened and how Mr. Lowenstein was really doing. The other part of me wanted to stay with the staff and residents who were so concerned about Mr. Lowenstein. Finally, I was on my way home. As I came through the garage into the backyard, I waved at Stella and Pamela, who were touring the garden. Stella was in her wheelchair and looked quite regal. I promised to join them shortly.

I ran upstairs and the first thing I checked was the answering machine. The light was blinking. The message was from Dan and it said to call him when I got home. I dialed his cell and again he answered on the first ring.

"Well, how did it go?" I asked impatiently.

"Like clockwork," said Dan.

"And how is Mr. Lowenstein?" I continued.

"He's a trooper," said Dan. "He took the fall and did an impressive job with those blood packets. I was really worried myself when I first saw him. You know he could have been hurt for real."

"I know, but he wasn't, was he?" I asked. "Dan, I need details!" It was like pulling teeth to get information from this guy.

"Well, it's not that easy to take a fall when you're 80," said Dan. "He has a few bruises and sprains, but no breaks, thank God."

"Thank God," I echoed. "And what did Iris and the attorney do?"

"Not a thing," said Dan. "The two of them really were in shock, I think. Iris may be cold blooded, but I don't think she much likes the sight of blood. Our people called in the '911' and got him to the hospital quickly. He's doing fine. If anyone goes in the room, he's on a set-up that really looks like he's on the breathing machine. Quite impressive."

"Now what?" I asked. "Just wait for Iris to make her move?"

"That's right," said Dan. "It shouldn't be long."

"Well thanks for the update and give Mr. Lowenstein my regards," I said. "He really is wonderful."

"I'll let him know what you said," said Dan. "You know he thinks that you're pretty special too."

"He said that?" I asked.

"He did. It takes a special person to work with the elderly," said Dan. "I know that. Isaac knows that too and he appreciates it."

"Well, thanks," I said, thinking what a lame response that was to the compliment. Why couldn't I be more glib? Like Tina. "I have to get going. Stella came home today and we're having a little celebration. Thanks again."

"Have fun," said Dan. "I'll give you an update tomorrow, or if something happens." He severed our connection without waiting for me to respond.

I'd been sitting on the edge of the couch while I was talking with Dan. I bent over, untied my shoelaces and slipped my shoes off. I knew I should think about going for a walk, as I'd been really lazy lately. All I really wanted to do was put my feet up and take a quick nap. I stretched out on the couch, but then I thought about how tight my jeans were starting to feel. I swung my feet over the side of the couch and dragged myself into the bedroom to change. I had the time for a quick walk before dinner.

It was a beautiful day. The sun was warm and the sky was a crisp blue. There was just a little chill in the air and a mild wind was blowing from the west. It was a perfect day to be out. And one thing I love about Jacobsport is that there are lots of great places to walk. It's easy to get to almost everything.

I walked my usual three miles, up to a little shopping center, then back down into the older part of town which is on the water and then home. It's a good walk uphill, downhill and level. It takes me about 45 minutes without any rush. Sometimes I think just going is as important, if not more so, than how far or how fast as it clears my head. When I got home I took a quick shower, slipped on some jeans and a sweater and went down to join Stella and Pamela for dinner.

"I am so happy to be home," said Stella, as Eugene jumped into her lap. "And Eugene is happy too, aren't you boy?" She hugged the cat, but he struggled and then bolted into the living room. He was back in minutes, however, and he barely left Stella's side the whole time I was there. Who says cats are indifferent?

"This lasagna is fantastic," I said to Pamela once we started dinner.

"Thanks," said Pamela. "It's really easy."

"Where's Charles tonight?" I asked.

"He's in Portland," said Pamela. "So I'm spending the night

with Mom." Stella agreed to have someone with her during the day, but she refused any help at night. She did agree to let Pamela stay the first night, however.

I reached for more salad and garlic bread, my contributions to Stella's favorite dinner. Stella was on a roll, giving us her impressions of what it was like to be a patient.

"Do you know how many times a day a nurse says 'just a minute'?" she asked.

"I have no idea," I replied. "How many?"

"I counted sixty-eight times one day," said Stella.

"Not just to you!" I said, "and not just one nurse."

"This was me listening to everyone," said Stella.

"I figure if one nurse says 'just a minute' five times an hour," said Stella, "times eight hours, times twelve nurses at Marian Manor, times three shifts, that's one thousand, four hundred and forty times in twenty-four hours just in this one place. Imagine if you added in all the hospitals and nursing homes and then added in nursing assistants and doctors! That has to be the most common phrase in the whole world! 'Just a minute'!"

"You had too much time on your hands at Marian Manor," I said, laughing. "We'll have to keep you busier here at home!"

I went back upstairs to my apartment about 10:00. There were no messages on the answering machine. I worried about Mr. Lowenstein, but I knew Dan would call if there were any changes. I quickly got ready for bed and brushed my teeth. I didn't even bother with TV. No sooner had I turned the off the lights than I fell sound asleep.

Sometime in the middle of the night, a loud blaring noise woke me. I couldn't figure out what it was, or where it was coming from. It was dark and I couldn't feel anything around me. Suddenly I realized that I wasn't dreaming. That horrible noise was my telephone. Whoever was on the other end was very patient, because it took me forever to find the phone.

"Nora, are you awake?" It was Dan. "Nora are you there?"

"I'm here," I mumbled.

"Nora, we got her!" Dan was elated.

"Got who?" I asked, like an idiot, having no idea what he meant.

"Nora, we got Iris!" exclaimed Dan. "Nora, are you awake?"

I shot up in bed. "I am now," I said. "What happened? What time is it?"

"It's about 2:00," said Dan. "Iris came in about 1:30. She said she couldn't sleep until she checked on Mr. Lowenstein. She said the accident was all her fault. Can you believe that?"

"Then what?" I asked.

"So the officer at the door to Isaac's room let her in and offered to give her some privacy," said Dan.

"Privacy?" I asked with contempt.

"It was part of the plan, Nora," said Dan patiently. "We posted a 'No Visitors' sign, but he was making a special exception for her."

"Sorry," I said. "Nice touch."

"May I continue?" asked Dan, pausing for several seconds. "So, Iris walked over to Isaac's bed and stood staring at him for a while. Then she disconnected the ventilator, picked up one of the extra pillows in the room and started to smother him. Of course, we were right there. And it's all on film. She protested for a while. Said she was just fixing his head to make him more comfortable. Can you believe it? Then she broke down and told us everything. She's been stealing from the residents for years, little things here and there, but valuable things. Recently, she decided that she had been doing so well with the little things, it was time to try for something bigger."

"The inheritances," I said.

"Right," said Dan. "The inheritances."

"So how is Mr. Lowenstein now?" I asked.

"He's great," said Dan. "He's anxious to get back to Marian Manor. He says no one gets any sleep in a hospital."

"And what about Iris?" I asked. "Did she need the money?"

"Not for any debt," said Dan. "She just got greedy. She wanted a better car. Better clothes. Better house. Sam just couldn't keep up with her. That was the conversation that you overheard that day in the library."

"What did she say about June Michaels?" I asked.

"Mrs. Michaels found Iris going through her closet," said Dan. "According to Iris, she felt that Mrs. Michaels was beginning to put two and two together. Iris knew it wouldn't be long until Mrs. Michaels figured out who was the thief. She had to get rid of June before that happened."

"Why didn't Mrs. Michaels say anything to one of us?" I asked. "She always told people that Iris was wonderful."

"Maybe she hadn't figured everything out," said Dan. "Or maybe she couldn't believe that Iris would do such a thing. I guess we'll never know."

"So Mrs. Michaels had made Marian Manor the beneficiary of her will," I said, "and she would want to change that if she thought Iris was a thief, right?"

"Now there's another reason for Iris to eliminate Mrs. Michaels," said Dan. "Marian Manor would come into money if Mrs. Michaels was dead. And if Mrs. Michaels did know about Iris, Iris had to get her before there was any chance to change that will."

"How did she do it?" I asked.

"Just as we suspected," said Dan. "She crushed up her own heart pills and mixed them in with a second dessert that evening. She knew that Mrs. Michaels never turned down anything sweet."

"How sad," I said. "I suppose she did the same thing to Harriet Allen, right?"

"We'll never know," said Dan. "Iris isn't talking about that one."

"What about Dominic and Tara?"

"Well it seems Dominic did steal a few things for Iris, but he didn't have anything to do with June Michaels' murder or the attempted murder of Isaac," said Dan. "Iris promised to help him get the money for school. It appears that Tara didn't do anything. She didn't even realize that anything was going on until they were at Tommy's pawnshop. Her only crime was in caring about Dominic and then not saying anything once she knew what was happening."

"Now what?" I asked.

"Well, Iris will be charged with murder, attempted murder and multiple thefts," said Dan. "She won't be coming back. Dominic and Tara will face some charges, but at this point, we don't know exactly how much they knew about what Iris was doing. They aren't likely to work in health care again, that's for sure."

"This is just great, Dan," I said. "Thanks so much for letting me know. Is there anything I need to do now?"

"Nothing at the moment," said Dan. "I'll be at Marian Manor in the morning, and we'll fill everyone in on what's happened. Thanks for your help, Nora."

"My pleasure," I said. After saying goodnight, I hung up the phone and lay there for a long while. I felt really good. The residents at Marian Manor were finally safe and I couldn't wait to see what happened tomorrow.

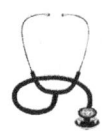

Chapter 22

"Hail, the conquering hero," shouted Herman Jessel when Isaac Lowentein returned to Marian Manor the next day. Mr. Lowenstein was blushing as Jean wheeled him onto 2 West, first thing the next morning.

"What's with the wheelchair?" asked Mr. Parker.

"I'm still a little stiff," replied Mr. Lowenstein. "Not as young as I used to be, you know." He laughed.

The happiness that everyone felt at Mr. Lowenstein's return was only slightly diminished by the sadness and disappointment of losing Dominic and Tara. We learned in report that the police had picked up these two after Iris spilled her guts. They would be held until their roles in this affair were certain.

"We want to hear the whole story," said Tina, "right down to those fake packets of blood. I think I'll wheel you into the dining room so everyone can hear."

"I hope this doesn't mean that you'll be leaving us, now that your work is done," said Charlotte Danner to Mr. Lowenstein. It was the first time I had heard her enter into a group conversation since June Michaels death. "I'm so grateful to you for finding out what happened to June," she added.

"It was fun," said Mr. Lowenstein, "and it was good to be needed again, but I think my days on the force are over. I have no intention of leaving Marian Manor. I still need a lot of help." Everyone started clapping.

Sam had called for a staff meeting that morning, so I left Mr. Lowenstein to tell his story while I finished passing morning meds. I knew I had to be particularly careful with the meds, because my mind was on all that had happened and I didn't want to make any mistakes.

When we got into the meeting, I saw that Sam, Dan, Cait and Dr. McCain were seated at a table in the front of the room. Mrs. Dixon was seated off to the left and Mr. Lowenstein had taken a chair in the front row. Staff came from all the units and there was standing room only.

Sam looked pale and haggard. His eyes were red rimmed as if he might have been crying. He called everyone to order and introduced those at the table. "I'll make this brief," he said. "I know you all have some of the facts, but I wanted to tell you myself that the problems we've been having are now, hopefully, resolved. Thanks to the good work of our police department, we've found the thieves who have been preying on our residents." He looked around the room, before continuing.

"I'm heartbroken to say my own wife Iris was the one most responsible and the one who took the life of June Michaels. She's now in police custody along with her brother Tommy. The police have also arrested Dominic Angelini and Tara Wilson, who were apparently helping Iris and Tommy.

"I can't tell you how sorry I am for what has happened. I've always tried to see that Marian Manor kept the spirit of my mother, who as many of you know, was committed to the care of the elderly. I'll be taking some time off and Mrs. Dixon will serve as the temporary administrator with the assistance of Bill Plankton from St. Andrews. I hope you'll give them your full cooperation. If you have any questions about this affair, Detective Maguire is here to answer them." With this, Sam left the room without talking to anyone else. He didn't appear to really see anyone anyway. Dan stood up.

"Before I answer any questions," he said, "I'd like to thank Sam and all the staff for their cooperation in solving this series of crimes. I also want to acknowledge the assistance of Isaac Lowenstein, without whom we couldn't have caught the people responsible. I want to thank Dr. McCain as well, because I know his reputation was on the line. Some of you didn't think he handled Mr. Lowenstein's 'stroke' appropriately. I hope that it's now clear why Dr. McCain did what he did." There were murmurs throughout the room.

"We also have to say thanks to Nora Brady for a number of things. It was Nora who figured out who the thieves were. She helped Isaac with his 'stroke' and she helped him get ready for the sting. So thanks, Nora." At that point Dan gave a little bow towards me and he started to clap. The rest of the room quickly joined him and I wanted to crawl under my chair.

"So what's going to happen to Iris, Dominic and Tara?" asked someone in the audience.

"That will be up to the District Attorney," said Dan.

"Has the police been able to recover any of the stolen goods?" asked another voice in the audience.

"Several things," Dan replied, "but these will likely be kept as evidence for the time being. We're still working on recovering the rest."

When the questions were finished, Dan asked if any of the others in his group wanted to add anything, but no one did. The room buzzed as people filed out. I tried to slip out without saying anything, but people kept jabbing my ribs or patting me on the back, with comments and questions like "Nice job, Nora," or "How did you figure it out?" I was completely embarrassed.

Back on the unit, Tina and Deborah were teasing me about having read too many Nancy Drew mysteries. Jean rescued me. "I think we need to have a little celebration today," she said. "I think I'll order pizzas for everyone at lunchtime."

"And what exactly are we celebrating?" I asked.

"We can celebrate Mr. Lowenstein's safe return," Jean replied. "We could also celebrate the fact that Mr. Jessel and Mr. Parker are brothers, even if the DNA results are not back. We could celebrate the fact that our residents can now rest easy regarding their possessions. We could celebrate the fact that the staff no longer has to be suspicious of each other and we could also celebrate the fact that you are, for the moment, not in trouble with anyone." She laughed at her last comment. I wasn't laughing, but I had to smile. "But most of all, we can celebrate that today is the best day we've had in ages."

"Sounds good to me," I said. Tina and Deborah were smiling and nodding their heads. Jean always says that 'tomorrow will be a better day.' It looked like "tomorrow" was finally here!

"12:30 O.K.?" asked Jean.

"Great," we chorused.

"What's great?" asked Kathy, coming up to bring residents down for one of the morning activities.

"I'm ordering pizza for everyone for lunch," said Jean. "You're invited, of course."

"What are you celebrating?" asked Kathy.

"One of you tell her," said Jean, laughing. "I can't go through that whole list again."

I rattled off the list for Kathy's benefit. "That's wonderful," she said, "but guess what?"

"What?" we all asked.

"I have more good news," she replied.

"Yes?" we asked again. "Don't keep us in suspense."

"I don't want to say just yet," said Kathy, "but I think it's certainly worth a special celebration."

"You just come on up at 12:30," said Jean, "and don't worry about anything else except bringing your good news."

And so the rest of the morning went very well. Dan and Cait stopped by on their way out. "Thanks again for your help, Nora," said Cait, waving as she walked on down the hall, leaving Dan at the nurses' station.

"Well, it's sure good to have this case behind us," said Dan.

"Yes," I agreed. "And I will be in touch about the charity golf tournament."

"Good," said Dan, turning to leave. "I'd like that."

"Someone's got a crush," crooned Tina softly as Dan walked away.

"I'm not sure which one of them is worse," said Deborah looking at Tina.

I smiled. "You two are nuts," I said, walking away. Today, I didn't care.

The pizza party was the celebration Jean had promised. Once the pizza was served, Kathy called for everyone's attention. "We just want to say again," she began, "how happy we are to have Mr. Lowenstein back with us safely. And I have another wonderful announcement."

"You're going to have a baby," someone shouted.

"No," she laughed, "but it's kind of related to that. Many of you know how John Parker has been working on tracing his family history. Well, guess where it led?" She pointed to Herman Jessel.

"You mean ..." Mr. Jessel pointed to himself and looked at Mr. Parker.

"It's true?" Mr. Parker looked at Kathy.

"It's true," said Kathy. "The DNA proves you two are brothers!" The two men hugged each other and again everyone in the room was clapping. Then everyone was crying.

I looked around the room and thought again of how much I enjoyed this job and how much I would miss all the residents and staff when I had to move on to the next assignment. I thought of how much I had learned since coming to Marian Manor. I knew the most important thing I had learned was that people grow old the way that they have lived their lives. I looked at the three amigos. Those who are lonely and self-centered when they are young will be lonely and miserable when they grow old. If people are happy and interested in other people when they are young, they remain happy, as they grow older. People never really change. I hoped I was one of the happy ones.

The End

Made in the USA
Monee, IL
02 May 2025